Make a Move, Sunny Park!

Jessica Kim

PRAISE FOR

Winter/Spring 2020 Indies Introduce Featured Title
Spring 2020 Kids' Indie Next List Selection
Amazon Best Books of the Month, March 2020 Selection
Kirkus Reviews **Best Children's Books of 2020 Selection**
Chicago Public Library Best Fiction for
Older Readers of 2020 Selection
Evanston Public Library Great Books for Kids 2020 Selection

★ "Kim has woven a pop song of immigrant struggle colliding with comedy and Korean barbecue." —*Kirkus Reviews*, starred review

★ "Kim has taught school, and it shows . . . with the spot-on dialogue. . . . This will certainly remind readers of Kelly Yang's *Front Desk* (2018)." —*Booklist*, starred review

★ "A must-read." —*School Library Connection*, starred review

"Yumi Chung . . . is a bona fide star."

—Booki Vivat, *New York Times* bestselling author of *Frazzled: Everyday Disasters and Impending Doom*

"A funny, tender story about family, friendship, and the courage to be yourself!"

—Karina Yan Glaser, *New York Times* bestselling author of the Vanderbeekers series

"Come for the puns, the laughs, and the wacky plot of mistaken identity, but it's the bighearted characters that take center stage in *Stand Up, Yumi Chung!*"

—Carlos Hernandez, author of *Sal and Gabi Break the Universe*

"I adored this book! Like, I seriously hugged it when I was done."

—Olugbemisola Rhuday-Perkovich, author of *8th Grade Superzero*, *Two Naomis*, and *Naomis Too*

"Yumi Chung is a headliner!"

—Remy Lai, author of *Pie in the Sky* and *Fly on the Wall*

Kokila
An imprint of Penguin Random House LLC, New York

First published in the United States of America by Kokila,
an imprint of Penguin Random House LLC, 2023

Visit us online at PenguinRandomHouse.com.

Library of Congress Cataloging-in-Publication Data
Names: Kim, Jessica, author. Title: Make a move, Sunny Park! / Jessica Kim.
Description: New York: Kokila, 2023. | Audience: Ages 9–12. | Audience: Grades 4–6. |
Summary: “From the author of Stand Up, Yumi Chung! comes a funny and utterly charming novel about friends—how to make them, how to let go of them, and how to be your own BFF”—Provided by publisher
Identifiers: LCCN 2022039237 (print) | LCCN 2022039238 (ebook) | ISBN9780525555001 (hardcover) | ISBN 9780525555018 (ebook) | Subjects: CYAC: Friendship—Fiction. | Korean Americans—Fiction
Classification: LCC PZ7.1.K5815 Mak 2023 (print) | LCC PZ7.1.K5815(ebook) | DDC [Fic]—dc23
LC record available at https://lccn.loc.gov/2022039237
LC ebook record available at https://lccn.loc.gov/2022039238

Printed in the United States of America

ISBN 9780525555001
1st Printing
LSCH

This book was edited by Joanna Cárdenas, copyedited by Betsy Uhrig, proofread by Misha Kydd, and designed by Asiya Ahmed. The production was supervised by Tabitha Dulla, Nicole Kiser, Ariela Rudy Zaltzman, and Caitlin Taylor.
The text is set in TT Tricks.

For anyone who's ever had a hard time
letting go of a friend

✧ Chapter 1 ✧

Three words: Inflatable. Dinosaur. Costume.

That's how I'll stand out from all the other people doing the Supreme Beat Dance Challenge on my social media feed.

It's so genius, I could smack myself. I mean, who wouldn't love seeing a giant T-rex getting down to the hottest K-pop dance track of the year? It's guaranteed to get clicks, maybe go viral, even. There's no way I won't win. Now it's just a matter of filming it, filtering it, captioning it, stickering it, hashtagging it, and posting it. Then it'll be in the bag.

Zipping myself in, I switch on the tiny fan, and the crinkly plastic quickly puffs up until it's as taut as a balloon. The strong chemical odor nearly makes me retch, but then I catch a glimpse of the ferocious six-foot-tall Tyrannosaurus rex looking back at me from the mirror, and I crack a smile. This is going to kill.

Peeking out from the underneath the dinosaur's mouth, I adjust my camera a final time to make sure the angles are all right before hitting play on my computer.

Sweat beads up on my brow as I scuttle to the cleared-out space in the middle of my bedroom. It's hotter than PE armpits in this costume, but I can't think about that. To collect myself, I take a deep breath before the song begins.

As soon as the first note of the frenetic trap beat drops, I'm a beast! The thumping cadence pulsates through my body as I sidestep and gyrate—a large lizard letting loose. The fact that no one will be able to see my face must have a freeing effect on me. My movements are so much bolder and more finessed now than in all my hours of practice!

Burning up and nearly out of breath, I'm just hitting my stride as the song launches into the dance break.

I'm busy body-rolling and booty-shaking when, out of nowhere, the door creaks open.

"Sunny?" a voice shouts over the pumping bass line.

I stop, whipping my giant dinosaur head around.

My best friend approaches, looking bewildered. “What are you doing in that thing?”

“Bailey?” Flustered, I unzip myself from the costume and emerge glistening with sweat. “Don’t mind me . . . I was just . . .” I slam my laptop closed, shutting off the camera and blaring music. “I wasn’t expecting you until later.”

In her text, she said she’d be coming over to show me something “very important.” She’s not supposed to be here for another fifteen minutes.

She picks up the now-deflated costume from the floor and tosses it on my bed. “Oh, right, I came a little early. Your grandma let me in,” she says with a smirk. “So what’s with all this, anyway? Halloween isn’t for two months.”

I let out a sheepish giggle. “It’s nothing. It’s just a video I’m making for this online dance challenge thing,” I reply, scooting my dinosaur costume hastily back into the box.

“Let me guess.” She taps her chin with her fingernail. “Does this have anything to do with your little Korean boy band?” she says with the slightest taunt in her voice.

"Maybe," I say, giving her arm a playful shove. "How'd you know, anyway?"

"What else could it be for? Look at this place!" Bailey spins in a circle, gesturing at my pale-pink walls, which are plastered with Supreme Beat posters. "You're obsessed with them, Sunny."

I straighten the albums that are arranged by release date on my shelf. "You say it like it's a bad thing."

She takes her backpack off and nestles into my desk chair, hugging her knees. "So you got dressed up as a dinosaur for a K-pop dance challenge, huh?"

"Well, it's not just any dance challenge," I rush to explain. "See, Supreme Beat is going to choose a select number of videos from the hashtag, and the winning picks get barricade tickets!" I point to the date triple-circled on my wall calendar. November 17: SUPREME BEAT CONCERT.

She blinks once, but her face doesn't move a muscle. "Cool."

Clearly she's not understanding the magnitude of what this means. "No, it's more than cool, it's amazing. Do you know how hard it is to get barricade tickets?

They're like five hundred dollars and they sell out as soon as they go on sale," I explain, getting myself worked up at the thought. "I really need to win them. It's my only chance to see Supreme Beat live."

Bailey gets up only to plunk herself onto my bed face-first. "Here I thought your whole K-pop infatuation would die by the time we hit middle school . . ." she says, her voice muffled by my pillow. "But it's only gotten worse."

"You know, if you gave it a chance, you might actually like it, too," I say, twisting a strand of my hair around my finger. "It's a lot of fun!"

"Sorry, but Supreme-whatever sound like they've had one too many Monster Energy drinks. They need to take it down a notch, in my humble opinion." Bailey scrunches her nose like she's diagnosing a foot fungus infection.

"They're not *all* like that. What did you think about the song I sent you last night?" I ask.

"Meh, it wasn't as bad as the others, but I don't know about the lyrics—what is that song even about?"

My eyes widen at her blasphemy. "It's called 'Precious'

and it's about friendship. It's actually pretty deep if you read the translation." I should know. I've learned every lyric of every song, including the Korean ones. Which is saying a lot because, despite the three years of Saturday language school my parents made me attend, I only have the skills of a kindergartener.

"Sorry, Sunny. Don't take this the wrong way. The song is cute, and I can see why you like it, since you're Korean and all." She stretches her arms back and clasps her fingers behind her head. "But I prefer music that's, you know, heavier, more mature."

Ugh. Not this "mature" stuff again. It might as well be a code word for all things boring and depressing. Not long ago, Bailey would have been down to do random stuff like dress up and dance around with me like a big dork, just for the fun of it. Like the time in fifth grade when we reenacted the whole story of *Frozen* using random vegetables from the fridge. Anna was a zucchini with orange yarn hair and Elsa was an eggplant with a Saran Wrap cape. It was hilarious.

But now that we're seventh graders, this would be unthinkable. All Bailey wants to do is talk about art or her emo poems or her bleak indie rock bands, and everything else is "babyish" in her "humble opinion."

Sometimes I miss the way things used to be.

"Supreme Beat's got other songs that are more mellow, too. I can send you links for those if you want," I offer.

"Eh, maybe." But she says it in a way that tells me she most definitely won't listen to them, which sucks but honestly doesn't surprise me much. That's Bailey for you. She likes what she likes and doesn't like what she doesn't like, and she rarely changes on either front. She's always been this way.

"So what's the big urgent news you needed to tell me in person, anyway?" I ask, changing the subject.

"Oh, right!" Bailey's eyes light up as she digs around in her backpack until she finds a packet of papers. "Check it out," she says, showing me the registration form for the Ranchito Mesa Middle School Dance Team tryouts.

"Huh? Since when have you ever been interested in joining the Dollies?" I ask, scanning the page. For the month that we've been at Ranchito Mesa, she's never had anything nice to say about them. I remember her going on a rant about how the name "Dollies" itself is exclusionary. Technically, the school officially changed it to the Dolphins to address that, but people have been slow to make the change. Do dolphins even dance?

She shoves my stuffed animals off my bed so she can scoot next to me. "What do you mean? I *love* to dance," she says with a pout. "Not that I'd ever admit this in front of my mom, but to be totally honest, I kind of miss dancing. A lot, actually."

"Me too," I confess. There's a sudden ache in my chest. It's been nine months since Bailey convinced me to quit ballet with her, but for some reason it feels like it's been so much longer.

"I figured." She hands me the packet. "Which is why I think trying out would be a really great opportunity. For the both of us!"

"Both of us? Really?" I bite the side of my lip. I don't know how I feel about that.

"Yes—not only could we dance together again, we could also get more plugged in to school stuff." She looks at me expectantly. "Maybe it's time we get out of our comfort zones and start interacting with other people for once."

"Oh." I give her a smile that isn't really a smile. I was under the impression she liked hanging out just the two of us. That's the way it's been since the third grade. Not that I'm against making more friends, but I can get really quiet and awkward around people I don't know. Maybe it's because I have social anxiety disorder, though my mom prefers to call it *overactive stranger danger.*

"I don't know, Bales," I start to say as heat creeps up my neck. "I usually try to avoid situations where people are staring at me, waiting for me to make a mistake." A sudden image of me jumping into toe-touchers while splitting my pants right down the crotch flashes before my eyes. "Yeah, I don't think so." I hand the application back to her.

Her eyes shoot up as she picks up on my escalating anxiety. "Sunny, you used to perform solos all the time in front of a bajillion people at our ballet recitals. This is nothing compared to that."

"That's different." Dancing in front of a dark auditorium full of cheering parents and grandparents is one thing, but dancing in front of a horde of judgy fellow middle schoolers in broad daylight is literally my worst nightmare.

"It's the same thing," Bailey says with a casual fling of her wrist. "Besides, it's not like you're going to be alone. There will be a bunch of other people dancing on the stage with you. Including me."

"Good point," I reply, my muscles relaxing a little bit. The thought of her being with me takes some of the edge off my nerves.

"We're getting older, and we should try new things." She clutches my pillow. "So, what do you say? Will you try out with me next week, then? I'll help you get ready." Her smile is so dazzling, her braces gleam in the lamplight. "Pretty please?"

Words don't come out of my mouth because my brain is still buffering. On one hand, everything about trying out makes me want to bury my head in the sand like an ostrich. But on the other, Bailey is begging me to do this, and I'd hate to disappoint her.

I wince. She gets so mad when I let her down.

"Hello? Anybody there?" Bailey waves her hand in front of my face, her eyes narrowing with a flicker of irritation. "C'mon, Sunny. Don't leave me hanging like every other person in my life has . . ." she says with a sharpness in her voice. "Are you in or not?"

The hairs on my arm stand up straight the way they do whenever I'm put on the spot.

"Uh, sure, why not?" I say, quickly relenting. "I'm in."

To my relief, the corners of Bailey's eyes crinkle as she grins. "Yay, I knew I could count on you!" she yells, nearly bowling me over in a giant bear hug. "I'm so glad we're doing this together."

"Me too," I say, our cheeks still smooshed together.

She releases me from her grip. "That's why I love you. You're so ride-or-die." Then she sticks her hand out at me. "Put 'er there, partner," she says in a faux cowboy accent.

I stop. "But didn't you say that you don't want to do this any—"

"Just not in public, you big dork!" She bops me in the ribs.

"Oh, got it," I say, grateful that it hasn't been totally banned like all the other things she's deemed "too immature."

We hold hands and do our secret handshake, bumping our forearms together and then our elbows before ending with an exaggerated shoulder shimmy shake while making a funny face. As usual, we collapse into a fit of giggles. I don't know what it is, but the scrunched nose and bugged-out eyes crack us up every time. We get up, jumping in circles, howling until we're clutching our stomachs, gasping for air as my cotton-candy-pink walls spin around us.

It feels so good to joke with her like this. It's almost like she's the old Bailey again.

Hope blooms within me.

Maybe if we make the team, it could be like this all the time.

Just like it used to be.

✧ Chapter 2 ✧

The next day, Bailey is over and we're helping my grandma make dumplings in the kitchen.

"Halmoni, why are yours so perfect and mine look like alien blobs?" I pinch the delicate wrapper into creases, concentrating on not tearing the dough.

"At least yours doesn't look like a turd," Bailey says, showing me hers, which admittedly does look like a little poop, especially the swirly part at the top.

I giggle as my grandma takes my misshapen dumpling, ignoring our shenanigans. "Girls, in Korean, we call it *mandu*," she says, refolding the wrapper so fast her fingers are a blur. "To have the nice shape, you must be patient and practice." She grabs all the finished ones from the bamboo basket with her chopsticks and throws them into the oiled pan with the tiniest flick.

The savory aroma of sesame oil wafting up from the stove makes my stomach rumble.

"In Korea, there is a saying that if you make ugly mandu, you will have ugly children," she explains, wiping down the granite countertop.

"What? Seriously?" I say with a snort. "Dang, that's harsh!"

Bailey tosses her mandu into the basket, and it lands with a thump. "Looks like my future offspring are in deep doo-doo, then!"

Halmoni keeps a straight face. "Look at your dad—he is okay now but maybe not so cute when he was a boy. Big head and big nose and big teeth and big glasses. Same as your uncle in San Jose and your aunt in LA. All ugly children!" She makes an unflattering face, scrunching her cheeks and flaring her nostrils. "But I keep practicing making mandu, and now they're not ugly anymore! Because of me."

I smack my forehead. My grandma has absolutely no filter whatsoever. Sometimes it's hard to believe that we're, in fact, related.

Bailey turns to me and mouths, "I love her."

Scooping crispy golden mandu onto our plates with her handy slotted spoon, Halmoni continues. "Eat a lot.

You need energy to practice for dance team tryouts."

I let out a sigh of dread. "Don't remind me. I'm so nervous I could hurl."

"You will be great. You are a good dancer like me." She gives me a whack on my arm. "Stop your negative thinking! Remember what the doctor said? Breathe and replace with positive thoughts."

To my horror, she closes her eyes and inhales slowly through her nose, demonstrating the calming technique we learned at the Coping with Social Anxiety workshop Mom made me go to a few months ago.

Luckily, when I glance over at Bailey to see her reaction, she's turned the other way, checking her phone. She doesn't even notice my grandma's exaggerated guttural breaths.

"Everything okay?" I ask, noticing the dark look that's come over her face.

"Ugh, it's my mom. She's on her way with Darren," she says, rolling her eyes at the mention of her mom's boyfriend.

"Uh-oh."

Bailey turns to my grandma. "I should get going.

Thanks for feeding me again, Halmoni," she says, botching the pronunciation so it sounds more like *harmony*. I've never bothered to correct her, and if I did now, it'd be too weird.

My grandma hands her a container full of mandu to go. "Take this with you. For later."

"Don't mind if I do." Bailey takes the Tupperware and gets up from the counter.

"Here, I'll walk you out," I offer, and we head over to the front door together.

"Can you believe my mom and Darren?" Bailey sits down on the floor to put on her chunky combat boots. "They might as well get their hips fused together!"

From the little I've seen, the guy seems normal enough—at worst he tries a little too hard—but Bailey hates his guts. And all his other internal organs, too.

"I wish he'd disappear . . ." But then her grimace transforms into a wide toothy grin. "Who knows, though? Maybe if I get on the Dollies, he will."

"Huh? What are you talking about?" I'm having trouble keeping up with Bailey's ever-changing moods.

"Think about it, Sunny." She pulls her backpack onto

her shoulders and tugs the straps with a sharp jerk. "If I'm on the dance team, my parents will have no choice but to come see me perform. Together."

"And?" What does this have to do with Darren?

"And who knows? Maybe some forced time together will make them want to work things out. Rekindle the love, maybe?" She makes an explosion gesture with her fingers. "And then poof, no more Darren."

"Ahhhh, I get it now," I say, not so much because I think her plan will work, but more because this explains Bailey's sudden desire to try out for the dance team. I should have known this was never about making new friends or whatever it was she said yesterday. This whole thing is yet another elaborate ploy to get her parents back together.

Though, honestly, I don't see it happening. From what I remember, Mr. and Mrs. Stern fought like cats and dogs. But what do I know? Maybe it'll be different this time around. There are actual Disney movies based on this very thing. Plus, if Bailey wants this so badly, then as her best friend, I should support her fully, right? Isn't that what best friends do for each other?

"Getting on the team will change everything for us," she says, pointing finger guns at me as she heads out the door.

After Bailey's gone, I can't help but feel concerned. Knowing her, she's going to be crushed if her plan doesn't work.

I guess I'm not the only one who is worried, because as soon as I'm back in the kitchen, Halmoni asks, "Is Bailey okay?"

I open the fridge and pull out a soda. "Yeah, I think so."

Halmoni's mouth straightens into a line. "So many changes in her family." She wipes down the counter with a small towel. "Must be hard."

"I'll say." It's dizzying even for me. This time last year, Bailey's parents were still married, and her mom was still an accountant who drove in our carpool to the ballet studio and sewed our recital costumes. Who would have ever guessed that by now, she'd be busting her butt running a cold-press juice bar up in the boonies with her hipster coworker-turned-boyfriend, Darren? It's a lot. No wonder all Bailey ever wants to do is hole up in her room and mope. "I think she misses her mom being around more," I add.

Halmoni puffs out a small sigh as she puts some more dumplings in the sizzling pan. "Takes time to get used to when someone is gone. You cannot erase pain, only wait for it to lift little by little."

It pinches when I realize Halmoni is probably speaking from her own experience. If anyone knows about absence, it's her. Last year, my grandpa lost his battle with cancer after being sick for a long time, leaving my grandma all alone after fifty years of marriage. After she lost a ton of weight, my dad got worried and convinced her to stay with us for a long visit. Lucky for me, she's liking it so much that she sold her house. Hopefully that means she'll be staying with us permanently.

When Halmoni first moved in, she kept to herself and slept a lot. The only time she wasn't sullen was when she saw Supreme Beat come on a variety show on the Korean channel. To cheer her up, I kept finding K-pop content for her and we'd dance together, and in time, she slowly crawled out of her sadness. I'll always be grateful to Supreme Beat for that.

She's much better now, but I know there are days that are still tough. Sometimes she goes on long walks by herself and comes back with swollen red eyes.

I don't want Halmoni to be reminded of any of that. "Guess what," I say to distract her. "My genius dinosaur costume idea didn't get picked for the Supreme Beat Dance Challenge."

Her mouth forms an *O*. "Jinjja?" she asks, shocked.

"I know. I thought for sure it'd win," I say, stuffing my mouth with another mandu. "I guess I'm not as original as I thought." When I searched the hashtag, I counted a total of fourteen posts that had inflatable costumes. Three sharks, one hot dog, three Pikachus, and seven dinosaurs.

"That's too bad," Halmoni says, helping herself to a mandu.

"I really wanted us to go to the concert," I whine. "Maybe it wasn't meant to be."

I'd been pinning all my hopes on this challenge ever since my parents refused to buy tickets. I think I could have convinced them if it were closer to home, but when they found out it's all the way in San Francisco, they were a hard no. Even when Halmoni offered to chaperone and pitch in to help out with the costs, my parents wouldn't hear of it. They said a couple of five-hundred-dollar tickets plus the cost of airfare plus hotel was too much for "someone my age." They told me the only way I could go is if I could find a way to pay for it myself, but I think they just said that knowing it'd be a lost cause. Maybe they were right.

Halmoni turns off the stove and brings the last of the mandu to the counter. "Don't give up so easily, Sunny-ya. If you want to go, you can find a way."

"But how?" I flop an uneaten mandu onto my plate with my chopsticks. "Even if I saved my allowance for a full year, it still wouldn't be enough to buy tickets. Two years, even."

"That's nothing!" Halmoni scoffs. "When I was your age, we were so poor that I used to make money by braiding my classmates' hair so I could go to dance class. And you are like me." She taps her temples. "Very determined. It's in our blood."

My grandma tells the best stories of when she was a kid. Like the time she snuck back and forth across the border during the Korean War to sell hard-boiled eggs to soldiers on both sides. Or the time she organized a betting ring for arm-wrestling contests to make money. Back in the day, she was a true hustler who played with danger like it was a game. Too bad I didn't inherit any of her fearlessness. The closest I get to living on the edge is when I drink milk on the date it expires.

She dips her dumpling in soy sauce. "There is always a way to make money; you just have to find it. Don't you know anyone who is good at selling things?"

I drum my fingers on the counter, racking my brain. "Now that you mention it, there's this girl who goes by @1SUPREMEbeaTZfan on the fan app. She's super popular for selling really cute handmade enamel pins. Maybe I can ask her for tips about how to set up my own business."

"Good start," Halmoni says with a look of approval.

The gears in my brain start whirring as I begin my research.

Looking for inspiration, I scroll through @1SUPREME-beaTZfan's website. She's got it all laid out: nice photos, cute descriptions, and packaging. I bet she makes buckets of money every week. Hopefully, she can give me some pointers.

As a rule, I don't start conversations with total strangers if I don't have to, but desperate times call for desperate measures. At least this is online and I don't have to interact face-to-face. To her, I'll just be @solarSBluv, another Supreme Beat fan from the app.

I can do this.

I just need to reach out to her.

Inhaling deeply through my nose, I count.

Five, four, three, two, one.

Here goes nothing.

Fingers tingling, I fire off a message to her.

If it'll help me get closer to getting those tickets, it's worth a try.

✧ Chapter 3 ✧

"Here it is, Sunny Bunny!" Dad says the next day as we walk around to where Mom is backing up a giant chassis attached to their truck. When your parents own and operate a parade float design business, you get used to all sorts of things pulling up in your yard. Today they're showing me the float prototype they've been preparing for their upcoming sponsors' meeting.

Dad whips off the tarp, revealing a fancy ballroom scene with four-feet-tall Styrofoam elephants frozen in mid-prance. "Just imagine it twice as large and covered in crepe paper."

"Looks awesome, Dad!" I say, genuinely impressed. I've seen the mock-ups, but seeing it in 3-D is totally different. "The chubby elephants are adorable. Love the design, Mom."

"Thanks, honey." She gives the float a good knock with her gloved hand. "I don't want to jinx it, but I think we've got a real chance to land the Kiwanis International contract and beat out C&C once and for all!" Mom says, fluttering her fingers together greedily like a cartoon villain.

Most people don't know that parade float builders are basically a bunch of rival nerd factions that live to one-up each other. There are only a handful of companies that do this, so they all know one another and compete for the same big contracts. Apparently, Kiwanis has the biggest budget of all the other sponsors and is thus the one everyone wants.

My parents' company, the Parade Brigade, lost the bid last year to C&C, and they've been on a mission to overthrow them ever since. It's a whole situation.

Recently, my dad, who used to be a software engineer, has been concentrating on creating cool techy features to edge out the competition. He's developed an augmented-reality app that lets parade-goers view the float in an interactive way from their phones, sort of like how the game Pokémon GO works. It's supposed to be their secret weapon.

"Prepare to experience the parade of the future!" he

says, using his faux news announcer voice as he pulls out his phone.

With great flourish, he taps the activate button on the screen.

We wait for something cool to happen.

But nothing does.

Uh-oh.

"Hmm, that's disappointing," Dad mutters, trotting over to check the signal receptor in the float's control panel. "The elephants are supposed to dance on the screen as merengue music plays."

"Why isn't it working?" Mom starts freaking out in typical Mom fashion. "We can't beat C&C with a dud app," she says, pacing nervously as Dad tinkers with the computers. "What are we going to do? The meeting is in a month!"

Clearly, I inherited my ability to stay cool under pressure from my mother.

"It might be the Bluetooth." Dad grunts as he pulls up a ladder and leans it against the device panel. "Sunny, can you go up there and reset the signal?"

"Sure," I say, climbing the nine-foot ladder.

"Great job, Sunny," Dad coaches from below, checking the analytics from his phone. "It's that one right there—careful of the live wires."

Gingerly, I poke my fingers between the snaking colored cords to tap the red button in the back of the panel.

"That's the one!" Dad says, giving me a thumbs-up. "Thanks, Sunny!"

I sigh. My parents' sense of danger is so warped. They're totally okay with me possibly electrocuting myself, welding steel poles, and manipulating Styrofoam while standing on scaffolding, but going to a concert in San Francisco with my grandma is "too dangerous"?

I don't understand them at all.

As I climb back down, something buzzes from my back pocket. It's the alarm I set for myself on my phone.

"Hopefully that'll fix it," I say, brushing the dust off my pants. "Now, if you'll excuse me, I have to go to Bailey's to practice for dance team tryouts."

Their heads swivel sharply in my direction, and their conversation comes to a screeching halt.

Dad's eyebrows shoot up into twin arches. "Did you say dance team tryouts?"

"Yeah," I say with a shrug, trying to keep it casual. I hate it when they make everything such a big deal. "Why do you look so surprised?"

Mom, stunned and blinking, replies, "You're not typically keen on doing new things with new people, what with your social anxiety and all."

I flinch. I wish she'd stop bringing it up all the time. Like it's the only thing that defines me or something.

She catches herself. "But I think that's a splendid idea! It'll be such a great opportunity for you to broaden your horizons and challenge yourself. Just like the doctor suggested at the workshop."

I resist the urge to roll my eyes even though I really want to.

"It's great that you're putting yourself out there, Sunny Bunny!" Dad says, giving me a hearty slap on the shoulder. "Atta girl!"

"It's not a huge thing." I shrug. "Bailey just thought it'd be a good way to make more friends."

Mom purses her lips. "Bailey? Is she trying out, too?"

I nod. "Why?"

"No reason." She shoots Dad a glance with bulging eyes. "I just want to make sure that this is something *you* want to do."

"What do you mean?" I scratch the nape of my neck. "Why would you ask that?"

Her lips twitch like she wants to say something. "Well, I know how pushy Bailey can be, and I don't want you to put yourself in another situation where you're going along with her just to go along with her."

I cross my arms. "When have I ever done that?"

Mom adjusts the platform for the Styrofoam elephants. "How about the time she pressured you to do the zombie escape room and you had to sleep in our bedroom with the bathroom light on for a solid week?"

"Oh, come on, that was forever ago." Six months at least.

Dad throws the blue tarp back over the prototype. "Or the time she gave you that 'hairstyle makeover,'" he says with air quotes.

My chest caves. In fifth grade, Bailey was inspired by something she saw on TikTok and was convinced that she could give me really sophisticated blunt bangs. They ended up so short, I looked like I got into a fight with a weed whacker. It took months to grow them back. Thank God for headbands.

Mom clears her throat. “Sunny, I think it’s fantastic that you’re trying out for the team, but you shouldn’t do it just because Bailey is doing it.” The setting sun casts a long shadow on half her face. “You don’t have to say yes to everything she suggests, you know.”

Ha! Clearly, Bailey Stern’s never been mad at her before, but I’d rather not get into all that again. She wouldn’t understand.

I kick pebbles on the concrete. “I’m not doing this for her. I want to do this for me. I think it’ll be fun.” I say it so convincingly, I almost fool myself.

“Well, then we support you one hundred percent.” Dad holds out his open arms for a hug. “Bring it in, bring it in!”

They wrap their arms around me, forming what we used to call a “Sunny Sandwich,” which was a lot cuter when I was little. Now that we are all about the same height, it’s just awkward, at least for me.

“As long as this is what you really want, I’m behind you.” Mom plants a kiss on the top of my head. “I’d hate for you to get steamrolled.”

“Thanks, but you don’t need to worry about me so much,” I say, wiggling free. “I’ll be fine.”

At least I think I will be.

✧ Chapter 4 ✧

Our school is laid out like a fan with all the wings converging in the center of campus, which is not the smartest design because it creates the worst human traffic jam at dismissal. It's easily the most stressful and chaotic part of my day.

Grabbing on to Bailey's backpack handle, I sidestep and weave my way through the throngs of backpacks, trying not to get trampled. Not an easy feat for someone who is only four foot ten.

"Guess what," Bailey asks, oblivious to the pack of soccer players that nearly mows me down. "Yesterday, I went downstairs to get a glass of water late at night, and I caught my dad watching the craziest thing on his laptop."

We make it past the quad, and I breathe a small sigh of relief as we get to the car pickup line in front of the school. "Oh yeah?"

There's a flash of mischief in her eyes. "Guess what it was," she says as she settles on the curb.

"Was he watching Supreme Beat music videos?" I ask, taking a wild stab at it.

"Ew, no! Why would you guess that?"

"I'm just kidding. Was it alien-abduction documentaries?" I try again. "Oh, wait! I know: Was it a true crime show?" Bailey got me hooked on those; it's so disturbing and addicting at the same time. "Remember the one where the guy forgets he's miked and confesses to the murders while he's in the bathroom?" A shiver runs down my spine. "So creepy."

Her cheeks puff up with annoyance. "No, now can you please let me tell the rest of the story?"

"Oh, sorry." Bailey hates when I get carried away. "What were you saying?"

"So, I caught my dad watching, of all things, his own wedding video." She covers her mouth with both hands, waiting for my reaction. "Isn't that so random?"

Just then, this annoying kid from my grade, Brenden, rushes past us, laughing maniacally as he grabs the hat off this skinny kid with glasses and throws it in the trash can as everyone watches. I shudder. That easily could have been me! Note to self: Do not, under any circumstances, wear a hat to school.

Bailey waves her hand in front of my face, snatching my attention right back to our conversation. “Hello? Are you even hearing me?”

“Oh, sorry. Yeah. What were you saying?”

Bailey draws closer to me and says in a low voice, “Something is up with my dad, Sunny. He’s not the type to watch old videos, especially not ones with my mom in them.”

“That is pretty weird,” I agree. It’d be an understatement to say that Bailey’s dad cannot stand Bailey’s mom. Not even that long ago, he was doing everything in his power to get full custody of Tic-Tac, their white Samoyed, just to spite her. Even though Mrs. Stern was the only one who ever fed him or walked him! Lucky for Tic-Tac, Mr. Stern got split custody, just like with Bailey.

“Are you thinking what I’m thinking?” She wiggles her eyebrows up and down.

“What?”

"Is this evidence that he misses her? Why else would he be watching that old video?"

She believes this so wholeheartedly that I start getting swayed myself.

"Maybe . . ." I scratch my chin, pondering. But it feels like a bit of a jump to make that conclusion.

"No, it has to be that!" Bailey shakes her head. "They've been separated a year now. Maybe he's starting to remember all the good times they had. Maybe he wants to get her back." She squeals, clapping her hands. "Wouldn't that be so cute, Sunny? It's a classic rom-com setup!"

Before I get a chance to weigh in, we're interrupted by a *beep beep* from Mrs. Stern's yellow Mini Cooper as it pulls up to the curb.

"Let's talk about this later," Bailey whispers before we crawl into the back seat together.

"Hi, girls! Sorry I'm late—the juice bar was slammed," Mrs. Stern says, running her fingers through her newly dyed bleach-blond hair. "Did you have a good day at school?"

I'm still not used to her look. Not just the hair color

but the butterfly tattoo on the back of her neck. This is a big change for someone who used to wear button-up blouses and slacks from Talbots. She's even switched back to her maiden name. Though it still feels strange to call her anything but "Mrs. Stern," so I've been avoiding addressing her altogether.

"Are you two ready for tryouts tomorrow?" she asks from behind her sunglasses in the rearview mirror.

"I think so," Bailey says, fastening her seat belt. "We've been practicing every single day."

"That's great, honey." Mrs. Stern reaches over to the passenger seat and hands Bailey a colorful gift bag filled with fluffy tissue paper. "I got a little something for both of you."

"What's this?" Bailey tears into the bag and pulls out two hair bows, one silver and one navy blue.

Her mom beams. "It's for tryouts. See? I got them in the official Ranchito Mesa colors!"

"Thanks," Bailey says, clearly unimpressed. School spirit isn't really her thing.

I take the silver bow. "That's so nice of you. Thank

you, Mrs. St— Uh . . ." My cheeks burn hot with embarrassment. "I mean Ms. Cordova."

"You're very welcome, Sunny," she says, her voice honey sweet. She takes a sip of her green smoothie. "When I heard that you girls are dancing again, I wanted to get you something to commemorate your comebacks."

Bailey rolls her eyes. "You mean *your* comeback," she murmurs under her breath.

I stifle a giggle.

Bailey's mom is one of those over-involved dance-mom types who's always fundraising, chaperoning, and volunteering to do makeup and hair backstage. Too bad for her, when Bailey quit ballet, she got cut off from that world. I can see why Mrs. Stern is so pumped about our tryouts. It may not be ballet, but this dance team thing would be right up her alley, too. I bet she's already got a Pinterest page dedicated to team T-shirts and matching swag bags. She is a sucker for matching anything.

As soon as we get to her mom's condo, I make a beeline for the bathroom, since I can't bring myself to use the toilets at school and my bladder is always ready to burst at this hour. "I'll meet you upstairs in a sec," I tell her through the door.

When I'm done, I'm headed upstairs to join Bailey, when her mom, who is preparing a snack for us in the kitchen, stops me.

"Sunny," she calls in a lowered voice, waving me over.

"Yes?" I reply. I'm suddenly nervous.

She glances down the hallway and then draws close. "I just want to thank you for being such a good friend to Bailey. I know the divorce has been tough on her, especially since I started seeing Darren, but she's really lucky that you're always there for her," she tells me in a near whisper.

"Oh, it's nothing," I say, brushing off her compliment. I don't know why, but for a second there, I thought I might be in trouble with her, which is ridiculous. I doubt Mrs. Stern has ever disciplined anyone in her whole life, not even Tic-Tac, who is still not completely potty trained.

"No, you don't understand. It's not nothing. The only time I see her laugh these days is when she's with you." Her bracelets clink as she squeezes my arm. "I know she can be a little demanding and clingy, but just know that it's because you're the only person she trusts."

I nod even though I've never once considered Bailey clingy. If anything, she's loyal. After being a total loner for half of elementary school, I've come to appreciate that she always saves a seat for me and waits for me after class.

"I hope you know how much she needs a friend right now." She covers her eyes with one hand. "Honestly, sometimes I think that if it weren't for you, she'd be completely lost."

"Oh, I doubt that, Mrs. . . . I mean Ms. Cordova, but thank you," I reply.

"Bailey is so lucky to have you." She hands me a plate of banana-oat cookies and veggie straws. "Here, take this up with you."

I climb the stairs with a new sense of responsibility. I always knew that Bailey counts on me for a lot, but now more than ever, I have to be there for her if I want her to go back to being her old self again, just like her mom said.

Even though it's already been a while now since Mrs.

Stern moved into the condo, Bailey's bedroom walls are still bare and her room is cluttered with half-unpacked boxes.

"What took so long?" she asks, putting on the thick reading glasses she's too embarrassed to wear at school. "I was starting to think you fell in the toilet or something."

I grimace, rubbing my stomach. "Sorry, I think it was the tuna salad from lunch," I fib, not wanting to explain my little talk with her mom. "Ready to start homework?"

"Sure," she says, tearing a piece of notebook paper from her binder.

I settle on the shaggy rug with my back against her bed and my binder on my lap. Carefully, I thumb through my student planner for the homework assignment.

"Seriously?" Bailey glances at the crinkled, stained pages of my planner. "You still haven't asked for a new one?"

I smooth out the page with my palm. "What? It's totally still usable!" I try not to draw any more attention to the spot where I spilled a whole glass of orange juice last week. Admittedly, it's been painfully embarrassing every time I've had to write down my assignments at the beginning of each period. Not only are the crispy pages super noisy, the whole planner is also starting to smell bad. The other day, Brenden Sylvester, who sits behind me in Social Studies, announced to the whole class, "Where's that gross rotten-orange smell coming from?" I wanted to crawl in a hole and stay there until I fossilized.

Bailey laughs, putting down her pen. "You are so stubborn, Sunny. There's literally a huge box full of brand-new planners in the office; all you have to do is ask the secretary and she'll give you one."

"I know," I say, fidgeting with my planner. "But you know I hate asking for stuff." Even now, my parents still order for me at restaurants.

"Well, here, happy birthday," she says, even though my birthday isn't for months. She pulls a brand-new student planner from inside her binder and tosses it to me. "I picked one up for you during my study hall, since I knew you'd keep putting it off and making excuses."

"Bailey!" I say, hugging it to my chest. "You did that for me?"

"Duh, I'm your best friend. Of course I did." She rolls her eyes, but in an affectionate way.

I'm speechless. "Thanks. I owe you one."

"Don't mention it," she says, already back to working on her algebra problem.

Just then, there's a ping from my phone.

There's a new message on my Supreme Beat fansite app. "Oooh!" I tap to open it.

"What is it?" Bailey asks, her back still turned to me.

"It's just my friend," I reply as I'm reading the message.

"Friend? Which friend?" Abruptly, she spins in her desk chair, craning her neck to see what I'm looking at.

"She's not from school. It's this girl I've been chatting with from the Supreme Beat fan message boards," I explain, slightly offended that having another friend is such earth-shattering news.

Bailey's long hair tickles my face as she hovers over me. "Who? What's her name?"

"Actually, I don't really know," I say while thumb-typing my reply to her message. "But her handle is @1SUPREMEbeaTZfan, and she makes really cute enamel pins."

Bailey grabs me by the sides of my face with both hands. "Sunny, don't you remember what we learned from the internet safety class at school? This person could be a stalker or a serial murderer for all you know! How can you call this total stranger a friend?"

I laugh, pulling away. She can be so dramatic. It must be all the true crime shows she watches on HBO. "It's not like that. We only talk about fan stuff."

That's the part I'm loving these days about being in the fandom. Since I started chatting on the message boards, I've been casually connecting with all kinds of people. Online, I'm not the Sunny Park who can't make eye contact and mumbles so quietly no one can understand. As @solarSBluv, I'm actually pretty normal—funny, even!

"Don't worry, it's super chill," I tell her.

"That's what all the victims say. . . ."

I giggle. "Don't worry, she doesn't know where I live or what I look like, so she can't stalk me."

"Yet you consider her a friend?" She nudges me with her toe.

"Oh, definitely! We've been chatting almost every

single day." Mostly about Kim Taeho, one of the lesser-known members of the seven-person band. He's shy and not as tall and good-looking as the others, but he's the lead dancer and also the one who writes all the lyrics, and we are both obsessed with him. "She's super hilarious and she always has the perfect GIF for every situation. You'd like her."

Bailey picks up her poetry notebook and pretends to leaf through it. "I have an idea. Maybe you should hang out with *me*, your actual friend, instead of your fake internet friend, who is probably some sketchy middle-aged dude who collects axes and lives in his mom's basement."

"She's not a middle-aged dude; she's in seventh grade, too." With a chuckle, I tuck my phone into my pocket. "Do I sense that someone is feeling a little jealous?"

"Ha!" Bailey puts her notebook down. "I'm not jealous, you dingus. I just want to finish this algebra assignment so we can practice dance." She bops my knee with hers.

"Sure." I bonk her back. I'd be lying if I said I didn't

enjoy watching her squirm with envy just a little. I guess in a weird way, it makes me feel special knowing that she doesn't want to share me with anyone else.

"Tryouts are tomorrow, if you haven't forgotten," she says. "Remember—we have to bring our A-game!"

✧ Chapter 5 ✧

At three o'clock on the dot, the final bell rings and it's go-time.

Gulp.

Tryouts, here I come, I guess.

I wipe my sweaty palms on my shorts and pack up my backpack, trying to counteract the fluttery feeling in my stomach with positive thoughts.

My heart races, so I take in a deep breath through my nose and hold it there in my chest before releasing it slowly. As I walk through the crowded halls, I force myself to be Zen, mentally reciting, *I will not fall on my face, I will not split my shorts, I will be fine* as I head over to the gym where I'm supposed to meet Bailey.

Turning into the PE wing, I notice that she's already sitting on the bench in front of the girls' locker room, waiting for me.

“You ready for this?” I call out to her, jumping into toe-touchers as I approach.

But when she looks up at me, I see that something is wrong.

Terribly wrong.

She’s not laughing. Her face looks stricken, and she’s been crying.

She shakes her head.

“Oh no, Bailey. What’s the matter?” I rush over and sit down next to her.

She doesn’t say anything right away, but then she flashes her phone at me to show me a text. It’s from her mom.

> **Mom:** You’ll never believe what just happened! Darren proposed! See you soon!

Below that is a photo of an elated Darren hugging Bailey’s mom around her neck. They’re still wearing their hairnets and aprons from the juice bar. She’s practically glowing, holding up her hand, freshly bedazzled with a diamond ring on her finger.

"Oh . . ." I'm so shocked, I don't have any other words. "Wow."

Bailey's eyes get glassy, and her voice cracks. "Sunny, she can't marry him." Her face is flushed, and tears stream down her cheeks in sheets. "This is not how it's supposed to go."

Quickly, I dig around my backpack until I find some tissues. I haven't seen her this upset since she first found out her parents were splitting up.

Passersby stare as she takes a big breath and blows her nose loudly into the tissue. "I didn't think they'd seriously consider getting *married*." She wipes her runny black eyeliner on her sleeves. "It's all so sudden. . . ."

I sit beside her quietly, letting her vent, not knowing what else I can do.

She buries her head in her arms. "I guess, deep down, I thought for sure that she'd wake up one day and realize how much she misses us and come back home." Her entire body heaves as she sobs. "I'm such an idiot for thinking that. Like my life is some kind of corny fairy tale or something."

I lean my head on her shoulder. "You're not an idiot, Bailey."

"How could she do this to me today of all days? She knows I have tryouts. How am I supposed to concentrate on dancing like this?" She laughs bitterly. "That's so like her. All she cares about is herself. She doesn't care about me or my dad. She's only concerned with her new life with Darren."

"No, don't say that. Your mom loves you, Bailey."

But she holds up her phone and shakes it violently. "Then why did she text me this? What did she expect? That I'd be happy for her? Congratulate her with some freaking emojis?" She stifles her sobs, pressing her palms over her eyes. "She didn't even have the decency to wait to tell me in person, after the tryouts are finished."

"Listen, Bailey, we can just go home if you're not up for it." I give her a hug, and she cries into my shoulder so hard, the wetness soaks through my shirt.

"You've got a lot going on right now, and the dance team is not a big deal compared to that," I offer in all earnestness. "We can always try out next year. Seriously."

Instantly, my brain kicks into overdrive, planning our next steps.

Halmoni should be finished with her Zumba class by now, and she could probably pick us up. I can take Bailey home and maybe put on one of those old black-and-white movies she likes, and we can drink her favorite Earl Grey tea until her dad comes home from work. Maybe she can write some poems. That might make her feel better.

But Bailey answers with a resolute "No."

She wipes her nose defiantly. "I want to do this. I have to do this."

"Are . . . are you sure?"

She doesn't look like she's in any kind of state to be dancing, or auditioning, no less. But I know better than to question her, especially when she's upset. When Bailey Stern sets her mind on something, there isn't much anyone can do about it.

"I'm positive." She steadies her breath and swipes her water bottle off the ground. "I'm not going to let my mom's drama stop me from living my life. She's done enough of that already, and I'm sick of it." She yanks her tote bag from the bench and flings it back onto her shoulder. "I refuse to let her or Darren take away another thing from me."

I stand up next to her, uncertain. "Okay, if you're sure that's what you want . . ."

"It is." Her face is determined. "Let's go."

I flinch when I check the time on my phone. "Oh no, we have to hurry, then. The tryouts started two minutes ago."

✧ Chapter 6 ✧

We sprint the length of the field as fast as our legs will carry us and get there just as a stocky lady—built like at tank and holding a clipboard—begins addressing the group.

"Hello, everyone, I'm Coach Tina. Welcome to the Ranchito Mesa Dollies tryouts!" she says in a booming voice, sticking a pen behind her ear.

I set down my backpack, trying to catch my breath.

"I'm so glad to see so many of you here today." Coach Tina shades her face with one hand and scans the place with eagle eyes.

I glance behind me, and my heart nearly stops when I realize just how many people showed up. Dang, everyone and their mama turned out for this.

I look over to see if Bailey is seeing what I'm seeing, but nope, she's looking straight ahead into the middle space, her face frozen. Like she's here, but she's not really *here*.

Uh-oh. Maybe it wasn't the right choice to go through with this, but it's too late now. It's okay. She'll shake it off as soon as the music comes on; she always does.

Coach Tina jams her clipboard under one armpit. "As you know, the Ranchito Dollies, ah, I mean Dolphins, are a serious dance team with a long tradition of excellence. More than that, we're a sisterhood." She stops abruptly like she just realized something. "Scratch that. What I mean to say is we are a peoplehood!"

She points her clipboard at the lone boy in the center of the group. "Sorry about that, Jadyn. I'm still working on fixing those gendered words."

Everyone turns to look at him, and he just waves shyly.

"I may be old, but I'm still learning!" She sticks her hands into the pockets of her navy-blue tracksuit and walks a few paces. "As I was saying, we're an incredibly competitive team and we're looking for the best of the best here today. So I sure hope you've been practicing, because that's what this team is all about: execution, consistency, and above all, no excuses," she says with fire in her eyes.

I can almost feel my knees knocking together. As if I wasn't already terrified. This coach is no joke.

"All right, folks, let me break down how this try-out is going to go." She points to the dirt track that encircles the football field. "In a moment, we're going to head over to that area over there, where you'll sign in and get your number. Please affix it to the front of your shirt. Then we'll split into two groups. Group A will do the freestyle portion first, then the choreographed routine, and then we'll switch and do it again for Group B." She clasps her hands behind her back. "Any questions?"

The boy, Jadyn, who was singled out earlier, raises his hand. "Any idea of when the results will be posted?" he asks eagerly.

Coach Tina rubs her chin. "I'm thinking, if everything goes well, we can have the team list up online sometime this weekend."

Eeek! That's so soon! My heart beats so fast, I fear it'll pound its way right through my chest.

The Jadyn kid, on the other hand, pumps his fist excitedly, like he's already made the team. Some people are born with all the confidence in the world. I wonder what that's like.

Coach lets out a hearty laugh, the kind that can only come from deep in your gut. "That's exactly the kind of energy I like to see." She points to everyone in the crowd. "Let me tell you something, folks. If you want to be a part of this team, if you really want to be a Ranchito Dolly . . . ah, Dolphin, you need to pour it all out on the line here today, capisce?"

"Capisce!" we reply in unison, already sounding like a team.

"All righty, then, let's get this party started!" She waves her arm, motioning for everyone to follow her.

Jittery energy runs high as we all migrate to the registration area together.

Over at the tables, I recognize the team captain, Lindsey Sorenson, handing out materials. She's one of the pretty, popular girls Bailey is always saying take too many selfies.

I turn to point her out, but Bailey's still in a daze.

"You okay?" I ask her cautiously. She's being unusually quiet, and I don't quite know what to make of it.

Bailey stares blankly. "My dad thinks my mom is going through a midlife crisis," she says out of nowhere.

"A what?" I glance back at her.

"You know, a midlife crisis. When old people start acting really reckless. That must be what's going on with her."

"Oh . . ." Dancers start forming lines in front of the tables, where they're handing out the identification numbers by last name. "You think?"

"Yeah, it's the only explanation," she says, like she's turning the theory over in her mind. "But honestly, if it is a midlife crisis, there's still hope that she'll snap out of it before the wedding. I mean, it's not like you stay in a midlife crisis forever, right?" She bites her thumbnail. "It's a phase, isn't it?"

"Maybe . . ." I walk with Bailey over to her table, struggling to listen as she talks. In my mind, I'm trying to figure out how I'm going to get over to my own line without cutting her off as she's pouring out her heart to me.

I check the time again. The lines get longer and longer, and I'm struck with terror. Under no circumstances do I want to face Coach Tina without my materials. Anxiety ripples through me at the thought of her screaming at me through her bullhorn in front of everyone.

I have to go. Like now.

"I'm really sorry, but I should probably go over to my own line," I blurt out, finally interrupting her. Though it comes out much louder and more abrupt than I meant for it to.

"Seriously?" Her eyes narrow into a scowl. "Sunny, were you even listening to me?"

"I was, I promise," I answer, startled by the edge in her voice.

She looks off into the distance, to where the soccer team is practicing on the other field. "You know, it's not easy for me to talk about this stuff with anyone, but since you're obviously too distracted to listen to me right now, I'll just stop," she says, worked up and red in the face.

Rattled, I clutch the hem of my shirt. "No, please don't. I'm sorry. I didn't mean to make you feel . . . I'll stay. What was it that you were saying?"

"Forget it," she mutters, looking past me. "Just go.

Since it's obvious that's what you want to do right now."

"No, really, it's fine; the line looks like it's moving fast. I'm still listening. . . ." I insist.

She glares right into my eyes. "I said forget it," she says, her tone hardening.

"All right," I say, unsure about what to do. "But as soon as the tryout is over, we can talk more about this, okay?"

She turns away. "Whatever."

Situations like this are so disorienting. It's hard to decipher what Bailey really wants from me sometimes.

Reluctantly, I walk over to my line, feeling like there are needles in my stomach. I should have known to stay with her while she was talking about her mom stuff. She's always so sensitive about it. What was I thinking?

I'm going over the million other ways I could have handled the situation, when suddenly I feel a tap on my shoulder.

✧ Chapter 7 ✧

"Um, excuse me," says a petite freckle-faced girl in bright-pink leggings and an oversize gym shirt.

I've seen her around; she's the only other kid at school who is as short as me. Despite her small stature, you can't miss her: She's got a bright-purple streak in her hair and a loud laugh that sounds like a goose's honk. She's usually bubbly and gregarious, but not today.

Grim-faced, she points to the front pocket of my backpack. "What up with your Supreme Beat pin?"

"What do you mean?" I turn around, surprised. She's the first person I've met from school who actually knows who Supreme Beat is, even though they're the biggest band in all of Asia.

"You copied my design." She twists around to show me the front of her own backpack, which holds a Supreme Beat pin identical to mine.

"Your design?" I break into a cold sweat. What is she talking about?

Her mouth flattens into a thin line. "You clearly ripped off my entire idea, and that's not cool. I spent a lot of time designing this."

Flustered, I back away. "I didn't copy you. I didn't even make this. I bought it from a girl online; she makes them and sells them on her website," I try to explain. "Her handle is @1SUPREMEbeaTZfan. Take it up with her." I feel a twinge of guilt, like I just threw my friend under the bus.

Her forehead wrinkles in confusion. "@1SUPREME-beaTZfan? But that's . . ." Her voice suddenly turns warm and friendly. "Wait, are you @solarSBluv?"

"How did you know that?" I whisper, and my back stiffens. This is getting weirder and weirder by the minute. First, she's alleging I stole her pin design, and now she knows my Fanverse username? I've never shared it with anyone on this entire planet except Halmoni.

She palms her forehead. "This makes total sense now." She points to herself with both thumbs. "I made that pin. I'm @1SUPREMEbeaTZfan!"

Shocked, I suck in a quick breath. "You are?" Could it really be her? Here?

"Yes!" She squeals, jumping up and down in the middle of the line. "Talk about random! I can't believe I'm meeting you in real life."

I'm stupefied that this is the girl I've been geeking out with over the past week! We've discussed everything from concept theories for upcoming album releases, to concert ticket prices, to song lyrics and what they might mean. Next to Bailey, she's my closest friend. Never in a million years did I think we'd ever meet like this.

"Sorry I thought you stole my designs, by the way. I get a little protective when it comes to my art," she says, running her hand through her hair sheepishly.

"Don't worry about it," I say, letting out a nervous laugh. "Honest mistake."

"This is so trippy, how well we know each other but we've never met. By the way, my real name is Beatrice, but my friends call me Bea," she says, chewing on her bubble gum.

"I'm Sunny," I say with a noticeable quiver in my

voice. I hope she's not disappointed by how timid I am in person compared to online.

"No way—Sunny?!" She starts cackling. "I get it now! @solarSBluv. *Solar* means sunny." Her laugh is squeaky and high-pitched, like a car's windshield wipers scraping dry glass. "Very punny."

Just then, the lady at the sign-in table waves me over. "Next!"

"Oh no, I should go," I say, suddenly realizing I'm holding up the line and everyone is staring at us.

"No worries! We'll catch up later over DMs!" Bea says, and we wave to each other. "Goodbye!"

After collecting my registration stuff, I can't shake the feeling that the world just got a little smaller. Who knows if there are even more Supreme Beat fans in my midst that I haven't met yet?

How awesome would it be if we all got on the dance team together? The three of us: me, Bea, and Bailey.

Oh shoot. That reminds me: Where's Bailey?

I find her on the opposite side of the field with the other group. From what I can tell, she looks all right, a little dazed, but at least she isn't crying anymore. She's smack-dab in the middle of the first line, which will put her right in front of the judges' table when she goes on, which actually might be good for her. Unlike me, she thrives under pressure and loves being center stage. I'm positive that once the music comes on, she'll snap right out of her funk. That's usually what happens when she dances. She'll be great. Just like she was in our practice sessions.

Maybe having a good audition is what she needs to take the sting out of her mom's news.

I cross my fingers tightly, hoping for the best.

✧ Chapter 8 ✧

When Coach Tina comes back, the din of excited chatter from the field fizzles into silence, and everyone gives her their full attention.

"All right, people, the moment you've been waiting for is finally here! If you haven't already, please find your positions so we can get started," she announces into the microphone, her amplified voice carrying mightily over the crowd.

As I wait for people to get to their spots, I'm so wound up with nerves, I feel like I might explode like a can of shaken soda.

Coach Tina stomps her foot to get our attention. "Looks like we're all sorted out." She clears her throat. "For the freestyle portion, you'll be evaluated on projection, precision, and creativity." She spreads her arm out toward my side of the field. "I don't have much to say other than try your best, and may the best dancers prevail! Group A, you're up!"

We shuffle onto the field and take our positions. I'm not quite ready when Coach Tina shouts, "Five, six, seven, eight!" and the booming beats of the audition track come on, triggering the adrenaline to course through my veins.

Instantly, the energy from this moment zaps me like a lightning bolt, and everything that was crowding my mind magically disappears. I'm no longer thinking about meeting Bea or whether or not I'll mess up my routine, or if Bailey is mad at me, or anything else. Right now, the only thing I feel is the beat pulsing through my body, telling me how to move.

I've practiced this freestyle routine so many times that my brain automatically goes into autopilot, and it's all muscle memory. That's the thing I love about dance. The way it pushes everything else to the sides so I don't have to think about anything—I can just *feel*.

Throughout the song, I'm vibing, swiveling my hips, swinging my arms, and busting out my favorite K-pop moves, completely engrossed in the moment.

When it's over, there's an immense release, as

if everything I was holding inside has finally been expressed, and it's freeing. It's been so long since I've felt like this!

I ride the high into the next portion: the choreographed routine. The music comes on over the loudspeakers, and I'm back in the zone, concentrating on nothing but executing the steps I've memorized in sync with all the other dancers around me. Miraculously, it goes without a hitch, and before I know it, it's over and we're switching sides.

Nervously, I sit in the grass on the sidelines, watching Bailey's group perform their freestyle routines on the dirt track. So far, she's doing great, twirling and leaping with sophistication and grace. As I'm watching, I can't help but notice how much shorter and smaller I am compared to almost everyone here. The only person around my height is Bea, who is doing a funky break dance. It's a little unexpected compared to Bailey's polished ballet, but I have to admit, that girl can really move!

The group is going into the choreographed portion when something catches my eye.

A few people in the front have broken formation.

They're dancing cautiously, with small movements, like they're trying to sidestep around something blocking the way.

That's weird.

I can't see much from where I am, so I try my best to ignore it.

It isn't until the song ends and the people disperse that I get a good look.

"Bailey?" I yelp, trying to keep my cool as I run over to her side. "Bailey? Are you okay?"

She's collapsed onto the ground. I can't see her face because she's buried her head in her arms. I throw my arm around her shoulders to block her from all the curious eyes. "Are you hurt? Did you twist your ankle?"

Bailey looks up when she hears my voice. "What if she really marries him, Sunny? What if she never comes back?" she asks, full-on sobbing.

"I . . . I don't know," I whisper, dumbfounded. I've always known my best friend to be dramatic from time to time, but in this case, I think it's real. She looks like she's completely lost it.

"Sorry, but I can't do this right now," Bailey says, her

body heaving with ragged breaths. "I need to go home."

"I know. It's okay," I reply, helping her up to her feet. "Let's get out of here."

She nods. Even though Bailey is almost a head taller than me, she looks so small and fragile right now.

Coach Tina comes jogging over, obviously worried. "What happened? Did you fall, honey?" she asks, surveying her and finding no obvious injuries.

Bailey shakes her head as people crowd around to see what all the fuss is about.

"She's fine. I'm her best friend, and she just . . . uh . . . she must have eaten something bad at lunch," I fib, trying to save face for Bailey. I go with the first thing that pops into my head. "You know how it is with tuna salad. All that mayonnaise. Gives her an upset stomach sometimes." What is up with me and tuna salad? Why is that, of all things, my go-to excuse?

"Yikes. I know what you mean—bad mayo can take out the best of us." Coach Tina shudders like she's reminded of her own past traumatic experience. "Are you sure you're okay?" she asks Bailey.

She wipes her eyes, trying to compose herself. "I'm

fine," she answers in a small voice. "I just want to go home."

"I'm not sure you're in any shape to be walking right now." Coach reaches to pull her phone out of her pocket. "Here, I'll call your mom so she can pick you up."

"Don't bother calling my mother," Bailey says, her voice tight. "I'm perfectly fine without her."

"Nonsense," Coach says, holding up her clipboard. "You can hardly stand up, let alone walk. It'll just take a second. I have everyone's contact info right here," she says, already flipping through her papers.

Bailey's eyes pool with tears again.

Her mom is literally the last person she needs right now.

"Actually, there's no need to do that," I insist, waving my arms. "I can make sure she gets home safely. We live really close by. Only two blocks over from here," I say, pointing my thumb behind me. "I think it'll be faster to walk home than wait to get picked up. She looks like she might need a toilet ASAP, if you catch my drift."

"You do have a point there," Coach agrees, studying Bailey's pallid complexion. She puts her hand on Bailey's forehead. “No fever yet, which is good. Listen, I want you to drink plenty of liquids when you get home. You need to flush that food poisoning right out. Gatorade is even better if you have it. You’re gonna need to replenish your electrolytes after you puke.”

Bailey just nods weakly.

“Take care of yourself,” Coach says, sending us off. “Remember: Replenish your electrolytes!”

The sun hangs low in the late-afternoon sky as Bailey and I grab our things from the bench and walk off the field together.

It isn’t until we’re around the corner that one of us finally says something.

“Thanks, Sunny.” Bailey’s voice quivers. “For staying with me.” She sniffs. “Even when I lose it.”

“I’m your best friend,” I tell her, letting bygones be bygones. “I’m always here for you. No matter what.”

✧ Chapter 9 ✧

Most of my Saturday is spent worrying about Bailey. She doesn't answer my texts or accept my FaceTime requests. I still have no idea how things went at dinner with her mom and Darren or how her dad took the engagement news or how she feels after tryouts.

When she finally texts, I bike over as soon as I can.

I walk into her room to find Bailey sitting on the carpet, brushing her dog, as depressing indie rock music plays in the background. Judging by the big cloud of floofy fur she's accumulated on her rug, she's been doing this for quite some time. Not that Tic-Tac is complaining. He looks like he's in doggie heaven, curled up in her lap with his eyes closed.

The poems Bailey keeps tacked up on her corkboard flutter as I brush past.

"Hey, Bales," I say, giving Tic-Tac a little pat on the head. He greets me with a warm lick on the hand before going back to his blissed-out state.

"Hey," she says with an air of nonchalance, like it's just another ordinary day.

"What do you mean *hey*?" I sink into her huge queen-size bed and clasp my hands under my chin. "I've been trying to get ahold of you since Friday. Why have you been ghosting me?"

"Sorry. You know Darren's Wi-Fi sucks up there in the hills," she says, flipping through the playlist on her phone to replace one bleak song with another.

"It's fine. I was just worried about you." Pulling in a deep breath, I ask, "So, are you feeling okay after . . . everything?"

Bailey pinches the fluff from the brush bristles. "Yeah. Why?" She doesn't even look up to meet my eyes.

Why is she being so evasive?

The words trip on themselves as they tumble out of my mouth. "I was just . . . I wanted to make sure you're good since . . . you know." I don't even know what to call it. The incident? The breakdown? "The tryouts."

There's a short pause.

"I don't know. It is what it is, right?" she says with a

dismissive shrug. "It's not like talking about it is going to change anything."

My heart shrinks in my chest. I can respect that, I guess. Maybe she's embarrassed, but I thought she might feel comfortable talking about it with *me*, of all people.

She pulls a folded-up piece of paper from her pocket. "I wrote a poem today. Want to hear it?"

"Sure." I sit up, giving her my full attention.

She clears her throat. "It's a haiku. Here it goes."

"Empty, turbulent

Drained of hope for reunion

How could you leave me?" she recites, enunciating each word slowly.

"Wow, Bailey. It's really deep and uh . . . profound." I wonder if she ever shares these with her parents.

She lights up. "Did you like how I paired the word *empty* with *turbulent*? They don't normally go together, so I thought it'd be a good contrast for the mood of the poem."

"Yeah, it really captured it. I think." I actually have no idea what she's talking about or what I'm talking about, but I'm nodding anyway.

"It's still not perfect, but it's getting there." She points behind her. "You want to go get a snack?"

"Sure," I say, just as both of our phones ding at the same time.

I gasp. It's an email from Coach Tina with the subject heading: Ranchito Mesa Dolphins Tryout Results.

Immediately, I tap to open it, and I'm shocked to see my name listed there next to Beatrice Papadakis and . . . Jadyn Reyes.

My stomach sinks. "Oh no."

I mean, I knew there was a slim-to-none chance that Bailey would make it, since she never finished her audition, but I was holding out a sliver of hope that maybe Coach Tina would make an exception and let Bailey on the team based on her references or past experience with ballet. Apparently she did not.

Nervous, I glance over to catch Bailey's reaction, but she's got her face buried in her dog's fur.

I lunge to hug her. "I'm so sorry. I—I know how much you wanted to make the team, and here I got on and you didn't . . ." I stammer.

"Sunny, stop. It's totally fine." Bailey jiggles out of my

grasp. "I'm actually glad that I didn't make it."

Her words stop me cold. "You are?"

"Totally." She scrunches her nose. "Just between us, all those dance team people are peppy and annoying, in my humble opinion."

My mind flashes to Bea and Jadyn. They're definitely peppy, but not in an annoying way, at least not to me. But maybe Bailey would think otherwise. After all, her idea of a good time is writing long poems about how much life sucks.

"You know the only reason I tried out for the team was to get my parents back together, and since that's not happening anymore, it's fine. Honestly, I dodged a bullet there."

The breath I was holding escapes. "Oh, good, because I was worried you'd be upset." I know how much she likes us doing everything together.

"I promise, you have nothing to worry about." She gives Tic-Tac a scratch behind the ears before getting up. "To be honest, I'm actually more worried about you!"

"Me? Why?" I sit up tall.

She pauses before sinking into her chair. "I know how

riled up you get when you have to do things by yourself, and it might be a lot with this team."

Goose bumps spring up on my arms.

Mindlessly, she traces her finger on the rim of the candle sitting on her desk. "All those pep rallies and performances in front of the whole school, not to mention the competitions. And to think that I won't even be there to help you through it all," she says with a wince.

Pressure coils around my ribs like rope. The crowds. The comments. The judgment. Suddenly, I feel lightheaded and short of breath.

She faces me. "That is, if you actually still want to go through with it."

My head cocks to the side. "You think I can back out now? Isn't it too late?"

"Absolutely not! Just because you got on the team doesn't mean you *have* to join."

It's like déjà vu. She said something similar when she convinced me to quit ballet.

She pushes her hair out of her face with both hands. "You could always decline. People do that all the time."

"That's true." I press down on my speeding heart with

my palm. Joining the Dollies was always Bailey's thing, not mine. If she's out, then there's no reason I have to subject myself to all this anxiety.

The only thing I'm bummed about is not getting the chance to spend more time with Bea. She seemed like a lot of fun, and I was looking forward to hanging out with her. But who am I kidding? She probably wouldn't have liked me anyway after she realized what a nervous wreck I actually am offline.

Bailey's voice goes soft. "I'm not going to tell you what to do. You have to do what feels right to you. I'm just saying, you have options." She comes over and swings her legs on top of mine. "Ask yourself if this team is worth going through all that for. You have to go with your gut on this."

It doesn't take me long to decide; my gut is crystal clear on this matter. "Okay, then, I'm not going to join the team."

Bailey nestles into her pillow, the tips of her lips curling like she's pleased. "Are you sure that's what you want?"

"Positive. Anyway, it just wouldn't be the same

without you." The tightness in my shoulders lifts. "You're my best friend, and we always stick together, remember?"

"Ride or die!" She wraps her arms around me and gives me a tight hug, laughing heartily. "OMG, so can I tell you how yesterday went? Talk about a dumpster fire, where do I even begin. . . ."

Before I know it, she's jabbering away, filling me in on all the details of her horrifically awkward dinner with her mom and Darren.

I exhale slowly, relieved that everything between us is back to normal.

Or so I thought.

✧ Chapter 10 ✧

I wouldn't go as far as to call my own mother "shady," but she definitely gets close when it comes to her parade floats.

"Where are we going?" I ask when I notice my mom making a left turn at the light instead of a right.

"Uh. I have a short errand I need to run before we go home. It'll only take a minute," she says, her eyes shifting side to side behind her aviator sunglasses.

It's obvious that she isn't telling the whole truth. "What kind of errand?"

"Let's just say it's for research, for work," she says, gripping the steering wheel and pulling into a half-empty parking lot. She hands me a beanie and sunglasses. "Here, wear these."

"Why? It's almost eighty degrees outside," I ask, baffled by her request.

That's when I notice that the parking lot we're in

directly faces the C&C warehouse. "Mom, are you serious? You're going to stalk your competitors?"

She pulls her hoodie up over her head and tugs the drawstrings tight so only a circle of her face shows. "Maybe."

"This is over the top." I scan the premises to make sure there are no security guards or cameras. There are none—in fact, there's nothing to see at all. "Isn't their float inside the building, though?" Unless she and Dad have developed x-ray vision (which actually wouldn't surprise me that much), we won't be able to see anything from here.

She winks at me. "Mr. Bakshi, the owner of the hardware store, mentioned that they'll be doing a large plywood delivery at C&C around this time, and I figured if we just happen to be here when they open their overhead sectional door, we might be able to catch a glimpse of their float."

I shake my head. My mother is on another level. I don't know why I'm still surprised by her competitive streak. This is the same person who regularly hides her Uno cards in her clothes or sometimes under couch cushions just so she can beat us. She doesn't play to lose.

"Don't worry." She takes the key out of the ignition. "It's not considered illegal trespassing, since we're on public property. I looked it up on the internet."

"Well, that's a relief," I say sarcastically. "What are you trying to see, anyway?"

"I'm just curious how they interpreted the artist rendition and how it stacks up against ours. That's all. Completely harmless."

"If you say so." I unbuckle my seat belt. "So now what?"

"Now we wait." She checks the time on her phone. "They should be here in ten minutes." She opens her purse and busts out a bunch of snacks.

Say what you will about my mom, but you'll never catch her unprepared.

"What's new with you?" She hands me a still-cold can of strawberry Milkis and a Choco Pie. "Have you heard back from the dance team yet?"

I set down my drink in the cup holder to let the bubbles settle. "Yeah, actually we got an email yesterday. . . ."

She nearly drops her bag of shrimp chips. "You did? Why didn't you tell me?"

"I was going to, but I fell asleep before you got home last night," I reply, even though it would probably be more accurate to say that I went to bed at eight to mentally prepare myself for the impending lecture about how I shouldn't let my social anxiety prevent me from living my best life.

"So, what were the results? Not that it matters either way." Mom holds her palm to her chest, clearly dying to hear the news. "You're a winner just for putting yourself out there; you should know that," she says, even though that's absolutely not how she lives.

I swallow so hard, a few chocolate crumbs get caught in my throat. "So, I got on the team, but—"

I don't get to finish because she erupts into squeals so high-pitched they could summon dolphins. "Congratulations, Sunny!" Her face beams with hope and pride. "I knew you could do it, honey. I'm so happy for you!"

"Thanks, but—" I start to say something to extinguish her enthusiasm, but she's so excited she doesn't even hear me.

"Now you can get back to dancing, you can meet more friends, and maybe even come out of your shell some. This is just what you needed, honey." She grabs her phone. "Let's call your father to tell him the news."

I shake my head vehemently. "Don't do that. Mom, listen to me," I scream so loudly, I finally pop her bubble of frenzy.

"What's wrong?" she asks, bewildered.

"Mom, I've been trying to tell you," I say, bracing myself for her disappointment. "I thought about it, and I'm actually not sure I want to be on the team anymore."

She frowns, lowering her phone. "But you worked so hard to try out. Isn't this what you wanted?"

Heat spreads through my body all the way to the tips of my ears. "I thought so, but I wonder if it'd be too much to be in a group that's always performing. The crowds and all that."

Her fingers grip her phone tightly. "But isn't dance one of the things that makes you feel at ease?"

"That was when I was little." My jaw tightens. "And this isn't the ballet studio; this is Ranchito Mesa Middle. Do you have any idea how judgmental people at my school are?"

She leans in and tousles my hair gently. "What are you worried they'll say, honey?"

Something about this question triggers me. It's clear that she doesn't have the slightest clue what I have to live through every single day. She still doesn't grasp that I have to fight against a tidal wave of negative thoughts that tell me lies about myself just to do stuff that's normal for everyone else. If she doesn't understand what I'm worried about, then she doesn't understand anything about me at all.

"I'm not just worried about what they'll say, I'm worried about every part of it!" I say, unleashing all the things that keep me up at night. "What if I mess up in front of everyone? What if I get majorly hurt? What if my teammates don't like me? What if I have a panic attack? Who am I going to hang out with now that Bailey's out?"

Mom's head tilts toward me. "Did you say that Bailey's out?"

"Yeah, she didn't make the team." I take a swig of my

strawberry Milkis, and the carbonation burns the back of my throat.

She blinks hard. "This is starting to make more sense," she says, almost to herself.

I put down my can. "What is that supposed to mean?"

Mom's eyebrows draw together. "Honey, do you think it's possible that you don't want to be on the team because Bailey isn't on the team?" she asks in a low, measured voice.

My head jerks sharply with a jolt of irritation. "No, that's not it. I don't want to be on the team for a lot of reasons," I say with exasperation in my voice. "I don't know why you have this thing against Bailey, anyway—she's literally my only friend."

Mom pauses as if she's collecting her thoughts. "Sunny, you know we adore Bailey and we always will, but I'm starting to see a very concerning pattern between you two."

"Like what?" I ask in a small voice, picking at a cuticle.

"Like ballet. You used to love going to class and doing recitals, and just when you got the solo for *The*

Nutcracker, you quit, right after Bailey did. . . ."

"Mom, I just didn't want to do ballet anymore." My voice takes a harder edge than I intend. "Is it so hard for you to believe that I grew out of it? You're aware that kind of thing happens at my age, right?"

She touches my hand. "Sunny, I know you don't like when I butt in when it comes to Bailey, but even between best friends, you still need to maintain healthy boundaries. You do not have to do everything together. It's okay for you to try new things and meet new people."

I pull away. "What if I don't want to meet new people?" Why is that a thing my parents assume I want? Has it ever occurred to them that I'm perfectly content the way I am? Not everyone needs a crowd to be happy. When will she realize that I'll never be the class president or a debate champ like she was when she was my age?

"Sunny, I think it's too early to quit the dance team if you haven't even given it a chance yet," she says gently.

"But I don't want to do it anymore," I say, unmoved.

"Give it one week, just one week to see how you feel,

and then you can decide what you want to do," she offers. "If you truly hate it, I won't give you a hard time about quitting."

Agitation builds in the silence between us until I can't take it anymore.

I look at her from the corner of my eye. "One week and you'll get off my back? You promise you'll stop bringing up how I quit ballet also?"

"Yes, pinkie promise." She holds out her finger.

If this means she'll stop blaming Bailey for everything, then fine. It'll be worth it.

We hook pinkies. "All right, but I don't know what the point is. I'm going to quit."

"Give it a chance. That's all I ask."

"Fine."

Just then, we're interrupted by the high-pitched squeak of a delivery truck hitting the air brakes.

"They're here!" Mom grabs a pair of binoculars from her purse and holds them up to her eyes. "This is it!"

The garage door rumbles open, and C&C's float stands in full view. They've got dancing elephants, too, but they took it in a more realistic direction compared to the cute cartoonish ones Mom made. It's almost a little too real and maybe a little creepy—not at all as playful and fun as the one my parents created. "It's just okay," I finally say. "Yours is way better."

Mom lowers the binoculars and starts cackling. "Not even close, C&C! You can kiss our butts!"

I laugh as I click my seat belt back in place. "Are you satisfied with your findings?"

"Oh yes. As far as I'm concerned, this Kiwanis contract is in the bag, baby!" Mom turns on the engine, and we peel out of there as fast as the minivan will go.

After dinner, I get into my fuzzy jammies and log on to my Fanverse account to catch up on the latest with Supreme Beat. I'm going through my inbox, replying to all the missed DMs, funny memes, and links to fan videos from my mutuals. It's hard to believe that a few weeks ago, I was just a lurker on this site of strangers, and now I'm getting concerned messages asking where I've been and why I haven't been on the message boards.

It's funny. At school, I could probably miss a whole month of classes before anyone would even notice, but here I'm gone two or three days and there's practically an online search party for me.

Though it wouldn't be accurate to call them strangers. We are much more than that at this point, even though most of us have never even been in the same time zone. With all the hours we spend chatting, maybe it'd be appropriate to call them friends, though that doesn't feel quite right either. Maybe they're somewhere in between.

That's another reason why I'm so eager to go to the Supreme Beat concert. I've read stories about people like me meeting up with their online friends at concerts and becoming friends even off screen. It makes sense, after all. The relationships are already there, so by the time they meet, it's a piece of cake. Just like what happened with me and Bea. Who knows how many more people I'd recognize and connect with at an actual concert?

My phone sounds with a notification.

It's Bailey.

> **Bailey:** What are you doing?
>
> **Me:** Nothing much, btw my mom is forcing me to try being on the dance team for a week before letting me quit.

Ack. I hold down the delete button with my thumb until the message disappears.

There's no way I can send this. I sound like a fussy toddler whose mommy is making me taste my lima beans before I can say I don't like them.

As if Bailey doesn't tease me enough about being immature for listening to Supreme Beat. Sending her this is just going to add fuel to the fire. I'm probably the only girl at Ranchito Mesa who still hasn't gotten her period—do I really need to be the seventh grader who needs her mommy and daddy's permission to quit the dance team on top of that?

Overwhelmed, I let my phone drop to the ground and give my laptop a face-shaped keyboard smash.

What am I supposed to do now?

The more I think about it, the more I wonder how necessary it is to tell Bailey about the agreement I have with Mom at all.

If I go to one practice like I promised Mom without telling Bailey and then quit right afterward, she won't even know the difference. Then I'll be spared the humiliation of my overprotective mom.

Brilliant.

Yes, that's what I'll do.

✧ Chapter 11 ✧

My insides jiggle like Jell-O as I head over to the school dance studio for the Dollies' first practice.

All day, I could hardly look Bailey in the eye knowing I had to keep this from her.

It royally sucks having to keep secrets from my best friend, but it's just easier this way. In any case, it'll be over soon, and I can forget that I ever tried out for this team in the first place.

My hands begin to tremble as I approach the practice studio, and I'm reminded once again why I avoid walking into rooms full of strangers at all costs.

I squeeze the soft fidget toy in my pocket a few times before opening the door.

Inside, it's pretty much just hardwood floors, a bar, mirrored walls, and the same distinct smell of old sweat and leather all dance studios manage to have. Groups of girls are gathered on the floor in threes and fours, chatting and giggling, and I've never been more intimidated.

They're all eighth graders and they're all wearing cute matching workout outfits. Being among these fully developed women makes me feel even more like a child than usual.

Slouching, I make a beeline for a spot near the door where no one is sitting, trying not to feel self-conscious about the baggy Supreme Beat T-shirt and ratty sweatpants I have on.

As everyone is busy catching up with one another, I warm up with some stretches. With my legs extended, I slowly reach over until I feel that satisfying pull.

"It'll be fine," I whisper to myself, releasing a breath. "I won't be here long enough for anyone to remember what I'm wearing. No one here really knows me any—"

Before I can complete my pep talk, the door swings open, and Bea and Jadyn come walking through, laughing and talking in animated tones.

Shoot.

"Sunny!" Bea yells, waving at me with both arms like she's trying to land an airplane.

Tension collects in my shoulders as I reluctantly wave back at her. I want her to come over and talk to me, but I'm supposed to get through this while keeping a low profile. It'd get so complicated having to explain everything about quitting. . . .

"Where the heck have you been, girl?" She sits down next to me.

Looks like I don't have much of a choice.

She pulls her shoulder-length hair into a ponytail. "I've been DMing you nonstop all weekend after I found out that we made the team!"

"I'm sorry. . . ." I wanted to reply to her, but I didn't know how to explain the deal I had made with my mom, so I didn't reply to any of her DMs. "I was pretty busy," I lie.

"No worries." She gestures to Jadyn, who has taken a seat next to her. "Have you two met yet?"

"I remember seeing you at tryouts. Sunny, right?" he says with a look of recognition. "I had a feeling you'd make the team. You were killing it out there!"

"Me?" I point to myself, giggling nervously. "No, no, no. I wasn't killing anything. I'm not a killer, by no means." My cheeks burn. "I mean, uh, thanks."

Quickly, I fold my hands in my lap because I don't know what else to do with them.

Why am I the most awkward person in the world?

I clear my throat. "So how do you know each other?" I say, trying to turn the attention away from me.

"Jadyn and I have second-period life science together," Bea explains.

He points his thumb in her direction mischievously. "Bea's always trying to be my lab partner so I'll do all the work," he jokes.

"Rude! We sit in alphabetical order," she says, punching him in the arm. "Anyway, you should be thankful I'm your lab partner. Without me, you wouldn't even know who Supreme Beat is."

I do a double take. "You're a Supreme Beat fan, too?"

"Yup, I converted him," Bea answers for him.

"More like she forced me," Jadyn teases. "Every time we did a lab together, she'd bug me to listen to this Supreme Beat song and watch the video. At first, I just ignored her, but then I got curious so I looked them up, and I realized what the hype was about."

Bea's lips curve up with satisfaction. "Told you you'd fall for them, too. Supreme Beat is irresistible."

Jadyn adjusts his glasses. "I stayed up until two in the morning streaming everything I could find."

"I did the same thing when I discovered them," I admit.

"Have you heard their new song?" He hums the melody of "Precious." "I don't know the words yet, but I can't stop listening to it. It's my favorite one on the album."

"Shut up! It's mine, too!" I clap my hand over my mouth. "Sorry, I didn't mean to tell you to shut up. . . ." My face burns red-hot.

"No worries, I totally get it," he says, waggling his fingers in my direction like he's casting a spell on me. "Supreme Beat has that effect on people."

"What about the dancing on the music video—wasn't it next level?" Bea says, rolling her shoulders, doing some of their signature moves.

"I know, right?" Halmoni and I spent so many hours watching them on YouTube on half speed to learn all the choreography.

"And the lyrics? The part about how friendship is delicate like a butterfly wing? I swear, Kim Taeho is a poet." Bea drapes the back of her wrist over her forehead in a dramatic swoon.

I nod. "He seriously is." A very cute poet, at that.

Bea says, "Fun fact. Did you know Sunny and I actually met on Fanverse before we met in real life at the tryouts? It's like we were meant to be friends. The universe brought us together."

Friends? *I* certainly considered us friends, but it feels good to hear that she feels the same way about me.

"I thought that kind of stuff only happens in movies!" Jadyn snaps his fingers. "That reminds me—I still need to ask my mom if I can sign up for my account on Fanverse."

Huh? Bailey had me thinking that I'm the only one on Earth who still has to ask my parents for permission for things like that. I wonder if he's not allowed to watch R-rated movies either.

"Yes, you must. That way we can start our own chat room. Sunny and I will teach you everything you need to know, right?" Bea turns to me with a small sigh.

"He doesn't know any of the fan chants, and he can barely name the members. We have our work cut out for us."

"Hey, hey, now," Jadyn says, patting the air like he's taming a tiger. "Don't discriminate because I'm new to this. We're all fans and we're dying to go to their concert just the same."

"Don't remind me about the concert! I want to see them so badly it hurts," Bea whines.

"I asked my mom if I could go, and she laughed in my face when I told her where it is," Jadyn says with a grimace. "It might as well be on Mars."

"Same," I say, and nod wistfully.

"Looks like we're all in the same boat." Bea puts a consoling hand on each of our shoulders. "At least on November seventeenth we'll be miserable missing out together," she says with a resigned sort of sigh.

I'm bummed, but it's also strangely comforting that they get the pain of this predicament, unlike Bailey, who just snickered when I tried to tell her about it.

Jadyn pipes up, "Maybe we can get together and watch the livestream!"

A tiny bubble of hope floats up in my chest. “That would be great.” Normally I don’t like to mix socially with people I just met, but in this case, it feels like the most natural thing in the world.

Right then, the door swings open and Coach Tina comes jogging in holding her clipboard.

✧ Chapter 12 ✧

The loud bleep of the whistle gets everyone to settle down. "Welcome to the first official Dollies practice of the season," Coach Tina shouts, her voice thundering off the studio walls.

"To start, let's meet our new recruits Jadyn, Bea, and Sunny. We're happy to have you join the Dolly family. I mean, Dolphins." She tips her visor at us. "You should be proud of yourselves; there were a lot of other dancers you beat out at last week's tryouts to be here."

Jadyn turns to give us high fives, and a big applause breaks out around me, making me feel like a total fraud. Like I'm trying on really expensive clothes that I have zero intention of buying.

"Since today is our first official practice, I thought it'd be nice if we could start with a game," Coach Tina explains, pacing slowly. "My personal philosophy is: We can't succeed together unless we trust each other, and we can't trust each other if we don't know each other. So that's the purpose of today's game: to get to know each other a little better."

My shoulders seize up. There's nothing worse than getting-to-know-you games. If it were up to me, Two Truths and a Lie would be renamed Three Lies That Were Carefully Chosen to Avoid Being Judged by An Intimidating Group of Strangers.

"To mix it up," Coach Tina says, swirling her index finger, "I'm going to separate you into random groups of four."

You've got to be kidding me. Now I won't even have Jadyn and Bea with me for moral support?

We split into groups, and I end up with Lindsey Sorenson, the prissy team captain, and two other eighth-grade girls: Mickey, the fast-talking one with big drawn-in eyebrows, and Tawni, the one with an undercut and orange sweatbands on her wrists.

This should be interesting.

Coach Tina passes out a poster paper and markers to each group. "Here's how the game goes. Basically, you will be racing the other teams to come up with a list of five things that you all have in common. Whichever team gets to five first wins."

I doubt there's even one thing I have in common with these people.

Coach rubs her hands together. "To make it worth your while, the winning group won't have to run laps during warm-ups."

Everyone erupts in cheers like the prize is a million dollars.

Mickey swipes the marker and points to us with it. "We're so winning this," she says with fire in her eyes. "Just follow my lead and we've got this!"

"Everyone ready?" Coach Tina blows her whistle. "Go!"

Before any of us even says a word, Mickey starts scrawling things on the list.

We go to Ranchito Mesa Middle School

We are on the dance team

Tawni turns her cap backward. "Why not add that we all have two legs and two arms while you're at it?"

Lindsey joins in the ribbing. "Yeah, isn't the point of this game to get to know each other better?"

Mickey lowers her eyelids in a challenge. "Are you saying you want to run laps, Sorenson? You like sweaty armpits? Smeared makeup? Is that what you're telling me?"

Lindsey gives her long blond hair a flip. "Ew, okay, no."

"Then let me be in charge here, you got that, selfie girl?" Mickey gives Lindsey a playful shove.

"All right, all right." Lindsey dodges out of the way, laughing. "Don't get your chonies in a bunch." She turns to me to explain. "That's the word we use for underwear in my family."

Just then, Lindsey bursts into snickers. "Remember when we were at regionals . . ." she starts to say but can't finish because she's laughing so hard.

It must be some kind of inside joke, because now Mickey and Tawni are giggling uncontrollably, too.

"Let me guess. You were going to tell Sunny about Chonie the Pony?" Mickey nudges me in the elbow. "For some reason, Lindsey started using *chonie* as a code name for our rivals the Mustangs. Something about how *chonie* rhymes with *pony*. I know, super random, but anyway, whenever we ran into them at the competition,

Lindsey would whisper *Choniiiiiie*!" Her voice gets high-pitched like a howling ghost's. "Just to be funny and make us laugh."

Tawni adds, "But it turns out that their coach's first name was Joanie, so every time Lindsey did it, Coach Joanie would look up to see who was calling her. She never figured out it was us."

Lindsey and Tawni clasp their hands together for a double high five.

Mickey cradles her forehead in her palm. "Welcome to the team; we're dorks."

I chuckle, both amused and relieved. Here I was feeling intimidated by these mature eighth graders, but it turns out that they're nothing but a bunch of goofs.

Mickey gives me and Tawni a good whack on the legs. "C'mon, we have to get our heads back in the game. I don't want to be running around that track on a hot day! We have to beat the others," she says, glancing nervously at the neighboring groups huddled together, whispering.

Slicking back her hair with her hands, Mickey makes a *humph* sound and turns back to the poster. "I know—

who here is the oldest of their siblings? I am and I know Lindsey is—anyone else?"

"I've got twelve minutes on Shawni." Tawni points to a girl in the group next to ours.

They're twins? Though now that I'm looking at them, it's pretty obvious. I mean, their names are Tawni and Shawni, for one. And they both have the same pointy chins and gravelly voices, even though they have totally different hairstyles and builds.

"Sunny?" Mickey calls, interrupting me from my thoughts. She turns her attention to me.

"Uh, sorry, I don't have any siblings," I reply, feeling guilty for breaking the group's momentum.

"Only child? I think that still counts, technically. Who says you can't be the oldest child of one?" Mickey adds it to the poster:

We are all the oldest child.

Lindsey and Tawni groan at how bad she's fudging the rules.

"Shut up—we only need two more!" Mickey says, frantically tapping the end of her marker on the poster. "There's got to be a faster way to do this."

"How about I'll say a bunch of facts about myself, and if you agree, raise your hand. I'll keep going until we find something we all share," Tawni offers.

"Sure."

She starts rattling off things about herself. "Let's see. I love the Los Angeles Dodgers. I have a pet hedgehog. I have a fear of clowns, oh, and also eyeballs, not when they're in the socket, just, you know, loose. Uh . . . I love every movie The Rock was in, I skateboard, and I get pineapple on pizza always."

No one raises their hand, not even once.

"Really? None of you are Hawaiian-pizza people?" Tawni says, scratching the back of her neck. "You guys are missing out."

"Okay, I don't hate Dwayne Johnson," Mickey says reluctantly.

"*Don't hate?* I don't think that's the same thing as *love*. . . ." Tawni says, slightly offended. "He's a comedic genius."

Mickey shushes her. "Sunny? Lindsey? Do you like his movies? Would you say they're above average?"

“Eh, the Jumanji movies were decent, sure,” Lindsey says with a less-than-enthusiastic shrug.

They all turn to look at me to confirm.

“To be honest, I haven’t really seen too many of them.” It’s embarrassing, but I had to shut off *Jumanji* in the middle. The stampede, the pelican, the booby traps, it was stressing me out too much. I never watched another one of his films again.

But when I notice the disappointment on their faces, I change my tune. “Actually, now that I think about it, I have. The Rock is awesome. Very funny,” I say with a huge smile plastered across my face.

“Sweet!” Mickey scribbles:

We love Dwayne Johnson movies.

“Let’s see, what else can I tell you about myself?” Tawni says, chewing on her lip.

“No offense, but you suck at this,” Mickey says. “Lindsey, you go next. Maybe you’ll do better.”

“Sure,” Lindsey says. “Is anyone else here into fashion? Beauty makeovers? Or photography? Celebrity lifestyle and pop culture? Reggaeton?”

Nope.

Her mouth bunches to one side. "Okay, surely everyone loves ice cream, right?"

Everyone raises their hands but Tawni.

"Can't. I'm lactose intolerant," she says, shaking her head with a grim face. "Ice cream gives me the farts."

I let out a yelp of a laugh. This girl seriously has no shame.

"What else is there? We just need one more thing we have in common!" Mickey says in sheer urgency as she looks around at the other groups. "Sunny, it's your turn. Start sharing. Quickly, just anything you can think of off the top of your head."

"Me?" There's a dropping sensation in my belly as the three of them stare at me, waiting for me to begin.

I draw in a breath. "Okay, sure, uh, so let's see. I like K-pop, I'm a Scorpio, I prefer dark meat to white meat on chicken, my favorite color is purple, I like my hot dogs with mustard, I have dimples. . . ."

To my surprise, I do better than the two before me. This time, hands actually go up and down, but so far, not all at once.

"C'mon, Sunny, you're doing great. Go faster!" Mickey urges, twirling her wrist. "Keep going!"

My heart races. "Right, okay, I've never been stung by a bee, I'm left-handed, I sleep on my side, I'm allergic to tree nuts, my shoe size is five and a half, I suffer from social anxiety, and I'm double-jointed!"

I bite my tongue, burning with the shame of a thousand suns. Did I really mention my social anxiety in front of all these people I just met? I've literally never shared that with anyone outside of my family and Bailey. I'm so embarrassed, I can hardly breathe.

"The last one! I think I saw everyone's hand go up for double-jointed," Mickey shouts, bending both her thumbs so they make ninety-degree angles.

"That's so cool! Look at mine!" Tawni yells, flipping her hand so her fingers lie flat on her wrists like she's got no bones. Meanwhile, Lindsey is pulling her elbows behind her back so they touch like butterfly wings.

"This is unbelievable!" She writes **We are all double-jointed** on the last line of the list and yells, "AHHHH! We got it! We won!"

Coach Tina comes over to verify our work. "Attention,

Dollies! It looks like we've got a winner!"

"Yay!" "We don't have to run laps!" "We won!" Swept up in the moment, our screams of victory overlap as we all jump around like we've won gold at the Olympics.

"Say cheese!" Lindsey busts out her phone and takes a group selfie of us.

"Great job, Sunny!" Tawni slaps her hand into mine in an aggressive high five. "Way to bring it at the end!"

"Thanks." I beam. I never thought I'd say this, but that game was actually a lot of fun and so are these teammates. Hopefully, in the wild chaos of winning, no one remembers anything I said about my anxiety.

When we're finally settled down, Coach Tina calls us back to attention. "Dollies, I hope you learned a few new things about your teammates. It's important that we keep finding connections with one another through the rest of the season.

"Before we start dancing, I've got a few announcements we need to discuss." Coach Tina glances at her clipboard. "The first order of business is a very exciting one. Can we get a drumroll, please?"

The Dollies start stomping their feet, making a

thundering sound that echoes off the hardwood floor. Bea and Jadyn join in, so I do, too.

"I'm very excited to announce that our regional competition will be held in just two months," she says, prompting cheers from the teammates.

Coach Tina grabs a stack of papers from a chair. "Here are some permission slips that I need your parents to fill out in the event that we win and qualify to go to state. I'm giving them out now because states will be held in the Bay Area this year, and I want to give your families plenty of time to make travel arrangements." She sticks her pen behind her ear. "If this season is anything like the last, we've got a good chance of going, so save those dates. Make sure these are signed and returned by the next meeting."

She begins to pass them around. "Let's take a five-minute break, capisce?"

"Capisce!" we all shout in one voice.

I head over to my backpack to put away my papers.

Bea gives me a pat on the back. "You're so lucky you don't have to run laps."

"I'm so jealous. The only time you'll catch me running

by choice is when I'm being—" Jadyn stops in the middle of his sentence. "You have got to be kidding me," he says, looking down at his permission slip like he's in a daze. "You've got to be freaking kidding me," he repeats.

Bea and I look over his shoulder. "What is it?" she asks.

"Did you see this?" He jabs his finger at the date and time printed on the paper. "It says here that the state competition is in San Francisco on November seventeenth! That's the same weekend as the Supreme Beat concert!" he squawks.

I hold the paper close. "OMG, you're right."

My heart stops in my chest.

"Do you know what this means?" Bea grabs me by the shoulders and gives me a hearty shake.

"We have an actual chance of getting to this concert!" I whisper, the realization sinking deep.

"Think about it. If we're already going to be in San Francisco for the competition, we won't have to pay for transportation or hotel." Jadyn's eyes are so big, they look like they might pop right out of their sockets.

"This is incredible!" Bea squeals, hopping on her toes

in a happy dance. "The only thing we need to figure out is how to get concert tickets!"

Coach Tina yells over the buzz of conversation in the studio. "You have one more minute!"

"We need to discuss this. How about we get together sometime after school to talk out the details?" Bea pulls out a sparkly purple phone covered in Supreme Beat stickers. "Does Thursday after school work?"

Wait, what?

"Yes, as long as it's after four. I have tap class until then," Jadyn says, checking his calendar app. "Is that okay with you, Sunny?"

I nod, and somehow, we're exchanging numbers. What is going on? Everything is happening so fast, my head is spinning. I'm supposed to be quitting this team after this week, not planning future hangouts!

"We can meet at my place. I'll text you the address later," Bea says, right as Coach Tina calls us back.

The rest of practice, Lindsey leads us through a series of stretches and combos, but in the back of my mind, I can't stop thinking about my situation.

If I quit the team, I won't have a way to go to the

concert, and worse, I won't have an excuse to keep hanging out with Jadyn and Bea.

A heaviness sits in my stomach at the thought of going back to being just a virtual friend or someone they once met.

Suddenly, I have second thoughts about everything.

I mean, would it be so terrible if I stayed on the team?

I'm liking it a whole lot better than I expected; the Dollies seem really friendly and fun, Jadyn and Bea and I have so much in common, and I really did miss dancing. I'm starting to think I might not want to quit after all, but then again, what would Bailey think?

Ugh.

✧ Chapter 13 ✧

After practice later that evening, I'm still trying to decide what to do about the dance team. I'm still no closer to an answer than I was before. The only thing that's changed is my hunger level.

I head to the kitchen in search of munchies, but I stop in my tracks when I see Halmoni in the backyard, dunking a head of Napa cabbage into a huge stainless-steel bowl of water.

I open the sliding glass door and slip on some flip-flops. "What are you doing out here?"

She pulls out the soggy-looking cabbage with her gloved hands and gives it a good shake. "Making the kimchi." She scoops some minced ginger, garlic, onion, and a porridge-looking substance into the big bowl. "Come help me."

"Sure." Curious, I pull up a chair next to her. I've never actually seen how kimchi is made. I put on a pair of rubber gloves. "Why are you outside, though? Wouldn't it be easier to make it in the kitchen?"

"Need big space. Messy."

Quickly, I see what she means, as red splatters fly when she starts vigorously mixing her sauce concoction with both hands.

"In old days, all the women in the village would get together in the yard to make the kimchi. Mom, grandma, auntie, neighbor, everybody helps. Sometimes takes all day."

"Holy cow." The sharp garlic smell stings my nostrils. "Sounds like a buttload of kimchi."

She makes an appalled clucking sound with her mouth. "They need buttload," she says, her face completely serious, "so they won't die!"

I hold the bag steady as my grandma pours a mountain of red-pepper powder into her sauce. "You know I love kimchi as much as anyone, but don't you think that's a little dramatic?"

"It's true. In Korea, winter is very cold. Cannot grow the vegetable because the ground is frozen. Not much to eat. So they had to make a lot of kimchi or they starve.

They put it in big jars and put them in the cool ground so it can stay fresh for many months. That's how they survived."

"That's intense."

She taps her temple with one finger. "Koreans preserve the food hundred years before refrigerator. Very smart. No matter what, the Korean will survive. It's in our blood."

"That's reassuring," I say, though I wonder if that gene skipped me somehow. Or maybe it doesn't apply to American-born Koreans. Bailey once said that I'd be the first one eaten in a zombie apocalypse because I'd probably feel sorry for the hungry zombies and surrender myself as their next meal.

My grandma pinches off a small leaf of cabbage coated in the kimchi sauce and holds it up to my mouth. "Taste."

I snarf it down hungrily. "Yum, that's good stuff."

Halmoni mashes the ingredients together with her gloved hands and slathers it onto the wilted cabbage leaves one by one. "Now we put in pot to ferment. Maybe ready by next Tuesday," she says, stuffing it into a tall glass jar. "You can eat it after your next dance team practice."

Unease bubbles up in my stomach like old kimchi. "Actually, I need your advice about that."

Halmoni stops pouring the kimchi juice into the jar. "What is it, Sunny-yah?"

I shift in my seat. "I was planning on quitting the Dollies after this week because I promised Mom I'd try it, but when I went to the first practice, I met some really nice kids. I didn't even get that nervous around them, and we had so much in common. These two, Jadyn and Bea, they even like Supreme Beat, too. Which made me think that maybe I might want to stay on the team. . . ."

"What is the problem?" she asks, smashing a head of cabbage into another glass jar.

I screw on the lid. "I don't know. This is the first time I'm doing something without Bailey, and I feel bad. Like I'm ditching her or something." Not to mention she sometimes gets mad if I hang out with other people too much. But I don't dare say that part out loud.

Halmoni packs the last bit of kimchi into the final jar. "Sunny, let me tell you a story."

She takes off her gloves and sets the jar aside on the table. "When your grandfather got sick, I stopped everything. I quit teaching dance class. Stopped going to church, didn't visit family or see friends. For five years, I only went to the doctor, prepared medicine, and took care of your grandfather. Everyone told me to see people, but I never listened. Missed your ballet recitals, your cousin's comedy show, and many other important things. When your grandpa died, I learned I could not have made him healthy, no matter how much I gave up." Her voice cracks just a little bit. "I don't want you to make the same mistake," she says with a faraway look in her eyes.

My heart tugs. She doesn't talk about my grandfather very often. "Halmoni . . ."

"Don't be like your stubborn grandma." She taps at her chest. "You want to help Bailey, I know, but quitting the team will not fix her problems." She touches my arm.

"Thanks, Halmoni," I say, even though I'm still not sure.

She doesn't know Bailey like I do.

Later that night, I get caught up doing what I always

do when something is on my mind: I clean. Anyway, Dad's been on my back about how I need to sift through my clothes for all the things I've outgrown. I might as well do it now.

I dump out everything from my dresser drawers into a huge mound in the middle of my closet and get to work sorting it into piles of things I want to keep, donate, and throw away.

It doesn't take me more than five minutes to get through half of it. I set aside jeans that are too small and a stack of T-shirts that I've long since outgrown. When I come upon an iridescent ivory chiffon gown, I freeze.

It's the costume I was supposed to wear for my *Nutcracker* recital!

Unable to resist, I hold it up to my nose and close my eyes, taking in the scent of it. I put it up against my body and check out my reflection in the mirror. It's still as pretty as ever. Touching the delicate satin ribbons brings back a flood of bittersweet memories.

I remember how ecstatic I was after learning that I got the part of Clara out of all the other girls in the conservatory. I can still picture my teacher congratulating me and handing me the costume in a gold shopping bag. It goes without saying I tried it on as soon as I got home, and I loved it so much I fell asleep in it that night.

It was also the day that Bailey found out that her mom was dating Darren. She was so furious with her that she quit ballet on the spot. She later told everyone that it was because she was over how "babyish" ballet was, but I suspect it was really her way of getting back at her mom.

For a while after that, she wasn't the same. She started getting really quiet, moping around her room, writing sad poems, and hardly said a word to anyone. As the date of the *Nutcracker* performance drew closer, I got busy with rehearsals and Bailey became even more testy and unpredictable. I know she was going through a lot with her parents, but there were some days that she was really mean to me. Sometimes she outright ignored me when I talked about *The Nutcracker*, like I wasn't even there. Other times she'd accuse me of doing ballet without her just to make her look bad in front of her mom, which wasn't the case at all. Every time I saw her, I felt like I was walking on eggshells but with soccer cleats on.

It got so bad that I started to have trouble sleeping at night. I didn't know how to prove to her that I was there for her, that I was on her side. No matter what I said, she wouldn't listen. That is, until I quit ballet myself two weeks before the performance. She was so impressed by my "ride-or-die" sacrifice. Then things finally got back to normal between us.

No one understood my decision, not even my parents, but I wasn't about to let that one performance get between me and Bailey. It wasn't worth it to lose her.

That's why I'm so conflicted about joining the dance team without her. I don't want her to take it the wrong way like she did with *The Nutcracker*. Like her mom said, she has serious issues trusting anyone but me. How would it make her feel if her own best friend left her, too?

At the same time, I can't help but be drawn to Bea and Jadyn. Being with them feels so easy and natural, like I've known them for years already. They're into what I'm into, and now we have a real chance of going to see Supreme Beat together. Live. That's an opportunity of a lifetime!

Walking away from that friendship feels wrong as well.

What am I supposed to do?

Overwhelmed, I shove all my clothes back into the dresser drawers and turn out the light.

My head hurts—I don't want to deal with all this right now.

I'm closing the closet door when something falls from the shelf and lands with a thud at my feet.

Reaching down to pick it up, I see that it's my old Magic 8 Ball!

What is it doing in here?

It's just a silly toy, but who knows? Maybe it can help me with my decision.

I shake it as hard as I can and squish my eyes shut. "Should I stay on the dance team?" I ask it, scared to read my fate.

With one eye open, I read the message in the triangle: **You must follow your heart.**

Ugh, I hate the vague ones. Why can't someone just give me clear-cut answers?

I flop onto my bed face first into my pillow.

What is *follow your heart* supposed to mean, anyway? Doesn't the Magic 8 Ball know that my heart is the most indecisive, second-guessing, wishy-washy organ in my whole body?

I toss it to the ground, and it rolls under my bed.

Defeated, I decide to call it a day.

I'm in the bathroom washing up when I get a message. It's Jadyn on our new group text.

Friends, my mom said I can start an account on the Supreme Beat Fanverse app! he writes.

Immediately, Bea replies, YES, YOU MUST JOIN US! YOU KNOW YOU WANT TO!

Should I? Jadyn asks, adding a string of heart emojis.

I gasp.

Follow your heart?

Heart emojis? Join us? You know you want to?

Once in a while, the universe answers the questions of your heart in the most undeniable ways.

I grab the Magic 8 Ball from under my bed. While I

have the attention of the powers that be, I decide to press my luck and ask another question.

I whisper, "Is Bailey going to be mad at me if I stay on the team?"

The blue triangle floats to the middle of the screen. **Better not tell you now.**

Wonderful.

Even the Magic 8 Ball knows how tricky Bailey can be.

✧ Chapter 14 ✧

"Bailey!" I call, running up to her in the cafeteria line. Usually we meet at the end of the quad after third period and walk to lunch together, but today she was nowhere to be found. "Where were you? How come you didn't wait for me?"

She tucks a wayward strand of hair behind her ear and looks past me at the growing line. "Sorry, I wanted to get here before the line gets long. Pizza day today."

"No worries," I say, a little unnerved, as I grab a tray from the stack. She's never left without me before, and she's being awfully quiet. There's definitely something up with her. I hope her parents aren't fighting again.

Bailey takes a bowl of fruit salad and a slice of cheese pizza from the cafeteria lady, but then she turns to me and looks me dead in the eyes. "I was waiting for you in the parking lot after school yesterday, but you never showed up. Did you go home sick or something?"

"Yesterday?" I grab my food, my hands clamming up. I must have been so nervous about going to the Dollies practice that I forgot to tell her not to wait for me after school. "No, no. I'm sorry—I guess I didn't get a chance to tell you . . ." I falter as we head out of the cafeteria.

"Tell me what?" she asks as we walk over to our usual spot on the other side of the quad, away from where all the "cool" kids like Lindsey Sorenson and her crew hang out.

I wasn't quite prepared to have this conversation, but I guess we're going to do it, right here, right now.

Carefully, I take a seat opposite her at the picnic table. "Actually, I was in the dance studio. At the Dollies practice." I spit out the words, finally coming clean, but it doesn't feel as good as I thought it would. In fact, it feels like I've admitted to committing a crime.

She frowns, and her head tilts to the side, like she might have heard me wrong. "What?"

I chuckle nervously, my throat feeling thick. "It's kind of a long story, but basically my mom made me go." I leave out the part about how it was supposed to only be for a week.

There's a long pause.

"She's making you stay on the team?" She snorts slightly and shakes her head.

I shift in my seat. "Yeah, she said something about how she doesn't want my anxiety to stop me from experiencing new things."

Bailey bristles as she pokes her straw into the milk carton. "That's so messed up. If you want to quit, she should let you. You're old enough to make your own decisions."

"You know how she is. . . ." I mumble.

She balls up the napkin in her hand, not having it. "Well, you could've at least told me earlier you were going so I didn't have to stand around waiting for you all afternoon."

I look down at my tray, suddenly feeling hot in my hoodie. "Sorry."

We eat in silence for a while.

"So how did it go, then?" Bailey finally says, folding her hands on the table, encouraging me to continue. "Your first dance team practice?"

"Kind of surprising, but actually it went fine," I reply, keeping it short and simple.

"Really?" Her eyebrows shoot up as she nibbles on an apple slice. "You weren't nervous? No panic attacks?"

"Nope." I peel the lid off my chocolate pudding. "Well, I was nervous, but, you know, that's normal for me."

She brushes her hair from her face. "How were the other new people? I saw from the email that Bea Papadakis made the team," she says, looking at me sideways. "She's the little girl from Mrs. Hortenson's homeroom, right? The one with the pterodactyl laugh?" She starts imitating Bea with a screechy laugh.

"I guess so," I reply, a little uncomfortable with her description.

She scoots in closer. "I saw you talking to her in line at tryouts. You seemed pretty chummy. Do you know her from somewhere?"

I bite my lip. She was watching me. "Yeah, actually, I know her from online."

She stops chewing. "Huh?"

"Yup, from the Supreme Beat fan app." I force my voice to sound casual and cool even though I'm anything but. "Remember? I told you about her. She's the one who makes the pins."

"That's her?" Her head jerks. "Shut up. Seriously?"

"I know—it was the most random thing ever." I take a big bite of my pizza.

Bailey smiles a thin smile. "That's great. At least there's someone on the team you know." She does not sound entirely sincere. "What about the other seventh grader?" She smirks, drumming her fingers on the table. "Jadyn something? He's the exotic-looking guy from tryouts, right? Kind of skinny and nerdy, with the thick glasses?"

"Jadyn Reyes," I reply. I don't know what's more offensive, the part about him being "nerdy" or "exotic-looking." The term *exotic* has always rubbed me the wrong way. Jadyn's got light-green eyes and brown skin, and that combo apparently means he's from somewhere else. It's like when people ask me where I'm from, even though I was born right here in Ranchito Mesa.

Bailey slurps up the last bit of milk from her carton, making a rattling sound. "Well, I hope things don't change between us now that you're officially a Dolly."

"What do you mean, Bales?" I reply, shading the sun from my eyes. "Why would anything change?"

"I don't know. I hope you don't get too busy for me,

that's all." She raises one shoulder and then lets it drop as she looks off into the distance. "Like everyone else in my life."

Later that afternoon, I'm still thinking about my conversation with Bailey as I do my homework in the living room. I feel terrible for letting her believe that Mom forced me to be on the team, but at least now she can't blame me for it.

It'll be tricky trying to balance it all, but I know how to deal with her. As long as I'm careful not to mention my Dolly stuff too much and let her do most of the talking, things will be fine.

I'm deep in my thoughts when I'm startled by a loud crash from the garage.

What was that?

Curious, I run over to check it out and find Halmoni standing on the top step of a ladder, surrounded by a bunch of boxes that must have fallen from the overhead storage rack.

"Halmoni, are you okay?" I ask, rushing to see if she's hurt.

"Ah, Sunny-ya. Don't worry, I'm fine," Halmoni says, wincing in pain as she rubs her leg.

"Ouch, what happened?" I hold the ladder steady and help her down.

She waves her hand back and forth to clear the dust. "I was trying to get this box out, but then everything fell down."

I recognize those boxes. They are the ones she brought with her from her house in Virginia.

"Maybe I am too strong!" She chuckles to herself as she wipes her hands on her pants. "Did you know your grandma can hold the plank the longest in the Zumba class?"

I help her stack the boxes. "What did you need from up here, anyway?"

"Ah, let me show you," Halmoni says, peeling the packing tape from the top of the box. She reaches into a small satin pouch and pulls out a beautiful jade pendant with long silken tassels and elaborate knots. "This is called a norigae. You wear it from the skirt of the Korean dress. My mother gave this to me when I was a young girl. It is for good luck."

I touch the smooth pale-green stone with my fingertips. "That's so cool, Halmoni. What do you need this for? Did you get invited to dance for another festival?" Every now and then, she gets called to perform traditional Korean dances for various events, but it's been a while since she last did one.

"No, I wanted to find this so I can give it to my favorite granddaughter." She play-punches me in the arm.

"Really?" My eyes go wide. I always had a suspicion I was her favorite, but she's never said it outright.

"Yes, I am going to Los Angeles to see your cousin Yumi's comedy show soon," Halmoni says with a twinkle in her eye. "Just a joke!"

"Halmoni," I groan, making a pouty face. "That's not funny!"

She slaps my hand lightly. "This is for you," she says, letting out a belly laugh. She places it in my palm, and the charm feels surprisingly heavy.

"Thank you." I trace my finger along its delicate edges. "But why are you giving this to me now?"

"I want you to have it so you can have good luck, too.

Since you are on dance team now, you will need it." She sighs deeply. "When you are my age, you want to give away your treasures while you can."

"Huh?"

She jolts like she just remembered I'm still in the room. "Never mind. You'll understand when you're older." She swipes at the air with one hand. "Come, let's go inside. Your parents are coming home soon. Almost time for dinner."

As we head back inside together, I can't help but wonder what she meant by *while you still can.*

✧ Chapter 15 ✧

That Thursday, I arrive at Bea's two-story townhome wound up with equal parts excitement and nervousness. Even though I've been texting with Jadyn and Bea all week, uncertainty still clatters inside me. There's nothing like unfamiliar surroundings to bring out my ultra-awkward side. That's probably why I rarely go over to anyone's house other than Bailey's. Well, that, and I've never really been invited until now.

Taking a deep breath, I ring the bell, but before it's even done chiming, the door flings open, nearly hitting me in the face.

"Yay, you're here!" Bea gushes, springing out of the house like a jack-in-the-box. "Come inside. Jadyn just got here, too."

Bea's warm welcome quells some of my nerves.

As I follow her through the hallway, the first thing that strikes me about her house is how welcoming and colorful it is, from the emerald-green walls to the cheery mosaic tiles that line the stairs. It even smells like cinnamon and warmth. It's exactly the kind of place I imagined her living in. It feels like at any moment, a troupe of gnomes and garden fairies might jump out of the corners and start singing a medley of encouraging tunes.

The sensory overload is a lot for me, but the moment I see all the Supreme Beat stuff in Bea's room, my nerves release like doves from a cage.

"It's like a shrine in here!" I gasp, taking in all the posters, figurines, and photo cards that fill her shelves. It's more merch than I have in my room and Halmoni's room combined.

Jadyn replies, "It's over the top, but in the best possible way, right?"

"Thank you." Bea settles down on her platform bed, which is decked out in a wacky pineapple print. "Should we get started on our business meeting?"

"Sure," Jadyn says, sinking into one of the oversize beanbag chairs.

I sit in the other one, eager to hear her money-making

plans. I bet she has all kinds of expertise in this sort of thing, as someone who already runs a successful enamel pin business.

"So the first thing we need to do is get permission from Coach Tina," she says, uncapping a purple gel pen.

"Actually, I have an update on that." Jadyn raises his hand high the way I imagine he does when he's in class. "I took the liberty of asking her about it after PE today."

"What'd she say?" Bea asks, her voice shrill with anticipation.

He pumps his fists in the air. "She said that we can go to the concert as long as it's after the competition and we have an adult chaperone to sign us out and supervise us."

"Awesome!" I pipe up. "I know—my grandma can be the chaperone. She's a huge Supreme Beat fan!"

"She is? That's so cute!" Bea coos in a pitch people usually only use for babies and puppies.

"Oh yeah, she's memorized all the songs and choreography with me. I'm sure she'd love to go." Normally I don't like to advertise how much time I spend hanging out with my grandma, but Jadyn and Bea don't seem like the types to judge.

"Great, it's decided: Sunny's grandma will chaperone." Bea jots it down in her notebook. "Looks like we'll be needing four tickets, then, including hers."

Jadyn adjusts his glasses. "Should we split the cost of her ticket, since she'll be chaperoning all of us?"

"That's fair." Bea does some long division on her paper. "That comes out to around six hundred eighty dollars per person, not including taxes and surcharges. To be safe, let's call it seven big ones."

Oof. Seven hundred dollars? "That's a lot of money," I mutter to myself.

Jadyn grabs Bea's Supreme Beat light stick from the bookshelf. "Yeah, but it'll be worth it. Imagine how much fun we'll have together!"

"Look, it's Bluetooth enabled." Bea slides the switch, and the light pulses in different colors. "At the concert, all the light sticks will be synched to the songs, and it'll blink to the beat!"

Jadyn stares at the light stick in his hand like it's suddenly enchanted. "What is this sorcery you speak of?"

“It’s true. I’ve seen some footage of concert videos online, and it looks like an ocean of color. Sometimes it even spells out a message,” I add.

“I’m dying to see that! Okay, we *have* to make this happen.” Bea looks back at her notebook. “Let’s brainstorm ways to make this money. Any ideas?”

“What about your enamel pin business?” I prod. “Can’t we help you make a ton of them and sell them on your website?”

Her mouth pulls down into a frown. “I don’t think so. You see, my pin business isn’t exactly profitable. I only make about a dollar and forty-nine cents per pin after I take out the cost of mailing and packaging.”

“That’s it?” I’d always wondered how the one I bought from her was such a good deal. My heart sinks. Earning seven hundred dollars per person in two months is starting to feel more and more out of reach. At this rate, Supreme Beat is going to be retired by the time we earn it all.

She shrugs. “Sorry, but I wasn’t making them for the money—it was more of a fun hobby to spread the Supreme Beat love.”

"What should we do to raise the money, then?" I ask, feeling increasingly out of my depth.

Jadyn drums his fingers on his kneecap. "Wouldn't it be smarter if we tried to raise the money however we can? We can do some things together, but we can also earn money doing chores and odd jobs on our own."

"So just hustle at our own rate?" Bea reiterates as she considers it. "Not a bad idea. I do some babysitting for my family already, but we could do some things together, too, and whatever money we raise, we'll split three ways."

"I'm down for whatever you guys think," I say. But honestly, I'd prefer it if we did everything together, though it looks like I'm the minority here. I can't even ask the school secretary for a replacement planner, how am I going to ask someone to hire me for work?

I drop my head in my hands. I'm screwed.

"I have an idea." Jadyn gets out his phone. "Let me check this website my mom uses called Greg's List. There are always posts for odd jobs in the neighborhood."

Bea and I watch over his shoulder as he scrolls

through the listings. “Oooh! This one pays two hundred bucks to shampoo someone’s carpet!”

“You can shampoo carpet? I thought shampoo was for hair,” Bea says, puzzled.

Jadyn shrugs. “I guess so, how different could carpet be? I’ve shampooed my sisters’ hair plenty of times.”

“You still bathe together?” I ask, a little disturbed.

Jadyn laughs. “It’s not like that. My mom runs a beauty salon in our garage, and we have one of those professional wash sinks back there.” He buffs his knuckles on his chest. “Not to brag, but my hair creations are something to behold. You could say I’ve picked up a thing or two being her helper over the years. In fact, I’ve done some pretty slick updos for all four of my sisters when they went to prom.”

“Wow, you have four sisters?” My mouth hangs open in shock.

He rolls his eyes. “Don’t remind me.”

Bea scribbles some math in her notebook. “Two hundred divided by three is sixty-six dollars and sixty cents. That’s a lot of money. Let’s do it!”

“But do you really think they’ll hire us for this job?

We're kids." I'm trying not to be a Debbie Downer about it, but it doesn't escape me that Bea and I are so short we could pass for fifth graders. We're not exactly what you picture when you think of professional carpet cleaners.

Jadyn rubs his chin. "Well, I don't see an age requirement anywhere in this listing."

"We'll be fine. I'll talk to them. Trust me, I'm good with adults," Bea says with a wink.

Actually, I could see her successfully talking herself into all kinds of situations. She could have a long and successful career as one of those infomercial people.

"And the worst that can happen is they turn us away, right? I say it's worth a shot," Jadyn says casually. "I'll send this person a message right now, and we'll see how it goes."

We'll see how it goes.

That's a hard thing for me to grasp. If it were up to me, I'd overthink every angle, come up with a bunch of terrifying worst-case scenarios, and ultimately chicken out. But it doesn't look like Jadyn and Bea will be backing down from this opportunity.

"Okay, sure," I say, trying to hide the quiver in my voice.

Jadyn taps away on his phone. "Done! I'll let you know when she replies."

"In the meantime, let me show you my most prized possession!" Bea gallops over to the bookshelf where she keeps her albums impeccably arranged in rainbow color order and plucks out a pale-blue one. "This is the one I was telling you both about in our chat. Ta-da!"

I gasp. "This is the autographed one?" I turn it over in my hands, staring at the squiggly signatures on the cover.

"Yup!" Bea does a little happy dance, jumping from foot to foot.

I hug it to my chest like it's a teddy bear. "I can't believe I'm holding something that's been touched by Kim Taeho!"

Jadyn draws close, taking a good look at each member. "Which one is he again?"

Bea's face falls. "Can you believe this guy? How can you not know which one Taeho is!" She pokes him in the chest hard. "Show a little respect. He's only the glue that holds this group together."

He yelps, looking over at me for help. "Can you tell her to stop harassing me, please?" he begs jokingly.

I stand up next to Bea in solidarity. "She's right, though. If you want to go to a Supreme Beat concert, you have to know the basics." I join in his public shaming. "Like Coach Tina says, 'Execution, consistency, and above all, no excuses!'" I say in my best baritone voice. "'Capisce?'"

Bea and Jadyn double over cracking up at my impersonation, which, I have to say, is pretty darn accurate, down to the way she points up to the sky for emphasis.

After we've calmed down from our antics, a sly look slips over Bea's face. "Don't you think that Taylor Tang from Mr. Patel's homeroom kind of looks like a seventh-grade version of Taeho?" There's an unmistakable swoon in her voice.

"Oh, you mean the boy you've been crushing on since school started?" Jadyn makes obnoxious smooching sounds.

I gasp. "Really, Bea?" He's not my type, but I could see

why Bea would be interested in him. He's got a lanky skater boy vibe that a lot of girls like.

Bea is appalled. "That's not true! Jadyn Reyes, you take that back right now. I do not have a crush on Taylor Tang!" She grabs a shaggy throw pillow from her bed and starts beating him with it. "Stop spreading your fake news!"

He uses his arms to block her surprisingly powerful blows. "That's quite a reaction for someone who doesn't have a crush!" he teases. "I guess since you're not interested in him, you don't care what he said to me about you today, then?"

She halts, her arm grasping the corner of the pillow midair. "What? He said something *about me*?" Her eyes bug out of her head. "You better tell me what he said right now!"

I'm rolling over laughing at her complete about-face. "Sounds like you might have a crush on him, Bea," I say.

Her face gets beet red. "Okay, maybe I do. But just a little one." She pinches her fingers a bit. "Both of you must swear on your lives and the lives of all seven members of Supreme Beat that you will never tell another soul about this."

We hook pinkies three ways to swear our secrecy. "Promise."

She leans in toward Jadyn. "Now, spill it. I want to hear every word of what he said about me."

"Fine." Jadyn says, "He said that your laugh is very cute."

She folds her hands over her heart and lets her body fall backward onto the bed dramatically. "He really said that?"

"Yup!" Jadyn draws a cross on his chest with his finger. "Cross my heart, hope to die. While we were waiting for our lab materials in science. Completely unprompted, too."

"This changes everything!" Bea sits up abruptly, new hope shining in her eyes. "Do you think I have a chance with him? I thought he was out of my league, but maybe not."

"What are you talking about? He one hundred percent isn't!" I reassure her. Bea's got charm that's fun and infectious. Taylor would be lucky to have someone like her in his life.

Bea tucks the pillow under her arm. "I heard a rumor that Brenda Sánchez likes him, too."

"Yeah, but did Taylor say that Brenda Sánchez's laugh is cute?" I poke her in the shoulder.

"Nope!" Jadyn shouts. "If I recall correctly, he said that about you!"

Bea flails her arms wildly. "He did, didn't he?"

We're deep in our analysis of Taylor Tang, discussing what Bea needs to do to get to know him better, when my phone buzzes in my pocket.

I reach to check it.

It's Bailey calling.

There's no way I can have a conversation with her here, it's way too loud. I mute the ringer.

I'll just call her back when I'm home. I'm having way too much fun here with Bea and Jadyn right now, and I don't want it to stop.

✧ Chapter 16 ✧

The thing about pimple cream is that it feels like someone is holding a lit match up to your zit right when you first dab it on, but if you can get through the moment of severe burning, it actually dries it up, and within a day it's totally gone. Dad saw this cream online and bought it for me months ago, but I never used it because I couldn't get past the stinging. Now that I know how powerful it is, I've learned to suck it up and push through.

It's been a revelation; my face has never been clearer.

In a way, I'm finding that my anxiety is like that, too. If I can tolerate the discomfort of tough situations, I can make friends, which is not something I thought I could do, at least not without Bailey.

After becoming a Dolly, I'm finding that the more I put myself out there, the more natural it becomes. It's definitely not easy, but I'm already so much more relaxed with Jadyn and Bea. For the first time in a long time, I feel like there's hope for me. I just need to keep at it.

I'm nearly finished dotting the pink ointment on my face with a Q-tip when there's a knock on the bathroom door.

"It's me!" I hear Mom's muffled voice from the other side.

I glance at the time on my phone. It's ten.

"Did you just get home now?" I ask, opening the door.

"Yes, sorry, work has been a mess lately." She takes off her bandanna and fixes her hair in the mirror behind me. "I don't know if I accidentally walked under a ladder or what, but we've had the worst string of luck all week."

"Uh-oh." I run water over my toothbrush and squeeze on some toothpaste. "What's going on?"

Her eyebrows pinch together as she plucks a few stray white hairs from around her temples. "Well, let's see. First, the suppliers sold out of floral sheeting and didn't bother to notify me about it until today. Then, when I was moving the generator, one of the Styrofoam hippos tipped over, and now it's dented. And then I found out the sponsors' meeting is all the way in Vegas this year, so I had to make flight reservations last minute and the rates were up the wazoo. It's been total chaos." She covers her ears with her hands. "I'm starting to think we're cursed. That Cynthia from C&C, I wouldn't put it past her to put a hex on us, honestly . . ."

I laugh, almost choking on my toothpaste. "I highly doubt that, Mom," I say, my mouth full of foam. Honestly, my mom is more apt to do something like that than the other way around.

"Well, I burned some sage around the workshop just in case," she says with a raised brow. "How're things going with you?"

I spit the toothpaste foam from my mouth and rinse the sink. "Pretty good. I met with my new dance team friends after school today to talk about Supreme Beat concert tickets."

She perks up like she's guzzled a can of Red Bull. "That's right, your grandma told me that was happening." She draws closer. "How did it go? Did you remember to bring your stress ball?"

"Yes, Mom, I did. Don't worry." I gargle mouthwash and spit.

"So tell me more. You weren't too anxious around

them, were you?" Mom's eyebrows draw together in concern.

"To be honest, I was pretty antsy at first, but then it was fine." I correct myself, "No, it was better than fine. It was great."

"Honey! I'm so happy to hear that!" Mom says, practically beaming. "And to think, you wouldn't have gotten to know them if I didn't force you to go to practice." She nudges me with her elbow.

"Thanks, I guess," I say, shrugging sheepishly.

"I had a feeling you might like being on the team if you gave it a chance." Mom fixes her gaze on me for a moment like she's about to get all mushy. She takes both of my hands in hers. "Look at you, growing up before my very eyes. My baby isn't a baby anymore, are you?"

Immediately, the walls come up and I pull away. "Please, Mom. Not this again." She should know by now that it makes me feel even more like a baby when she talks to me like this.

Her face softens. "I'm sorry. Am I being too much?"

I nod.

She holds up her palm like she's taking an oath. "From

now on, I'm going to try my hardest to not be so— What is it that you're always saying? Twitchy?"

"Not twitchy!" I say with a snort. "Cringey!"

"Right, that's the word. I'm not going to be *cringey*!"

"I appreciate it, Mom."

Then her eyes catch on the shiny norigae I left on the counter. "Wow, isn't this Halmoni's hanbok charm? It used to be your dad's grandma's." She turns it over in her hand adoringly. "I haven't seen this in years."

"It is. Halmoni gave it to me." I wipe my face on a towel.

"She did?" Mom remarks, her forehead puckering in confusion. "Why?"

"I don't know, she said something about how she wants to give it to me while she still can. It was really random."

"I see. . . . I just assumed she'd do that later . . ." she starts to say but then stops herself as if she's said too much.

"What do you mean 'later'?" I repeat.

She forces a smile and looks the other away. "Oh, nothing, honey. I just thought she'd, uh, wait until you're older, that's all. Since you're not going to wear your hanbok anytime soon."

She ruffles my hair, but her eyes are darting back and forth like she's trying to figure out what to say next. "You know what, I'm actually feeling pretty beat. Like I said, long day." She stretches her arms out and yawns. "I'm going to get ready for bed myself."

That was abrupt.

"Okay, good night, I guess."

"Night!" She plants a kiss on my cheek. "Don't stay up too late, okay?" she says, slipping past me down the hallway to her room.

Something is up with my grandma, and Mom definitely knows about it.

What is it that she's not telling me and why?

The next day before second period, Bailey approaches me in the hallway, skipping gleefully.

"Sunny, I have huge news," she tells me, bouncing on her toes. "Huge."

"What is it?" I can already tell it has something to do with her parents. That's the only thing that can bring out emotions this big in her.

She grabs me by the elbow and leans in like she's

going to tell me a secret. “Darren is cheating on my mom!” she blurts out.

We turn into the PE wing. “Oh no, are you serious? How did you find out?”

Her eyes intensify, and she starts talking really fast. “Yesterday I was over at my mom’s after going wedding dress shopping, and he got a call and excused himself to the other room, saying it was for work, but when I was passing by the door, I overheard him saying ‘Hey, baby, I haven’t heard from you in ages!’” she imitates in a deep voice.

I gasp. “Really?”

“Yup, so I got curious and stuck around to listen in, and right before he hung up, he said ‘I love you; can’t wait to see you again soon.’”

My mouth drops open. It doesn’t sound like she’s jumping to conclusions this time.

“I know. What a lying, cheating little turd!” she says with a clenched jaw. “I knew something was off about him. He sends creepy vibes from a mile away.”

“That’s so terrible for your mom, though.” I remember how swept up Mrs. Stern got in the whirlwind of romance when she first got together with Darren. It was a weird time. Not even a month after the divorce, she bought the juice bar, and a few months later, she's basically living with Darren. For weeks, she was dancing on air, playing cheesy love songs and saying all this stuff about destiny and fate. This is going to be gutting for her.

"Terrible?" Bailey snorts. "What are you talking about? This is the best news ever! Once she finds out about him, she'll dump him once and for all."

"You haven't told her, then?"

"Not yet. I don't want to say anything until I have some hard evidence. That's why I called you yesterday, but you never picked up," she says, looking at me from the corner of her eye as we pass through the crowded halls.

I curl my backpack strap tightly around my finger. "Oh, that's right! I'm so sorry. I meant to call you back, but I forgot," I say, letting out a stilted ha-ha.

She swings open the locker room door, and we're hit with the unmistakable whiff of sweaty socks. "Let me guess. You were at another dance team thing?" she asks with an edge in her voice as we walk inside.

"Yup. How'd you know?" I busy myself, securing my backpack on the hook inside my locker. I know my meeting with Jadyn and Bea wasn't technically a dance thing, but I can't very well tell her that we met to talk about Supreme Beat concert tickets. Then she'd just say some garbage about how immature we are. She's already biased against the Dollies; I don't want to give her more reasons to dislike them. The less she knows, the better.

"Can you come over after school on Tuesday? I want you to help me come up with a plan to trap Darren." She spins the combination on her lock and yanks it open.

"No, I can't. Sorry, I have practice." I strategically arrange my PE clothes on the bench. Carefully, I pull my arms out of my sleeves and grab my PE shirt and stuff my head inside, trying to hide as much of my exposed body as possible.

Bailey whips off her clothes and tosses them into the bottom of her locker. She stands in the middle of the locker room in just her bra and underwear without an ounce of self-consciousness. "Ugh, fine." She rolls her eyes. "Go hang out with Jadyn and Bea, then. Again."

"Sorry."

"Whatever." She puts on her uniform, but then a mischievous look appears on her face. "Hey, Sunny. Guess who I am?" Out of nowhere, she starts laughing wildly, throwing her head back while making a weird high-pitched screeching sound that I recognize immediately.

It's Bea's laugh.

"Bailey! Stop that!" I jump up on the bench and try to cover her mouth with my hand, which only makes her laugh more and do it louder. "You can't do that!"

Horrified, I'm practically wrestling with her to get her to stop as people from all over the locker room gawk at us to see what the fuss is about.

"C'mon, Bailey. That's mean," I beg, trying to get her to cut it out, but she is having too much fun.

"It was just a joke," she says, still laughing. "I didn't realize you were so protective of your new friend. It's like you two are besties or something," she says with a challenge in her voice.

"What? Not even!" I say, offended that she'd suggest such a thing. "She's just my teammate, that's all."

"Right." Bailey smirks, sounding a lot less jokey than just a moment ago. "You sure are spending a lot more time with your 'teammate' than you are your own best friend these days," she says with finger quotes.

Silence stands between us as we walk out together to the yard, where we're supposed to be doing warm-up stretches.

My chest tightens. I can tell by the way she's acting that if I don't say something fast, this is going to turn into a big deal.

I shift my feet. "I know what you mean, though. Sometimes she does kind of laugh like that, doesn't she?"

Bailey's face brightens. "It's not just me, right?" The corners of her lips turn up impishly as she hooks her arm into mine. "You noticed it, too?"

"Yeah. A little." I nod, grateful that the tension has broken.

"You know how she makes this air horn sound," she says, demonstrating that awful noise again. "I bet you could do it better than me, since your voice is higher. Come on, try it once," she urges me, grabbing me by the arm.

"No, no," I say, shaking my head. "I can't." That would be so messed up.

"Sunny, look around. It's just me and you here. It's not like she can hear you from wherever she is," she says, pointing to the wide-open space at the back of the PE warm-up area. "Don't be such a baby about it. Just do it for me." She's exasperated now.

I sigh, rubbing my forehead in my hands. It's clear she's not going to leave me alone until I do this.

I look to my right and to my left to verify that no one is in earshot.

Quickly, I make the window-wiper sound, which cracks Bailey up so uncontrollably that she accidentally lets out a giant fart, which sends us both into hysterical fits of giggles.

We're laughing so hard that we're grabbing our stomachs, crying.

Bailey wipes the corner of her eye. "That was too funny. I haven't laughed like that in forever."

"Me neither." But when the laughter fades, it's slowly replaced by something that doesn't feel very good.

Luckily, Bea will never find out about this.

✧ Chapter 17 ✧

The next Tuesday after school, I'm sprinting through campus, leaping over hedges, trying to make it to dance team practice on time. I got caught listening to another one of Bailey's never-ending rants about how her mom's become a total stress case between running the juice bar and planning her wedding. She was so worked up, I couldn't get a word in edgewise to tell her I had to go. Why do I always get stuck in these kinds of situations?

Wet with fresh sweat, I finally make it to the studio and creep through the open door as stealth-mode as I can, but the room is already strangely quiet.

Everyone's gathered around Coach Tina.

I start to panic. *Did they already start? Am I the last to arrive?*

"So good of you to finally join us, Sunny," Coach Tina says, checking her watch.

Jadyn, Bea, Lindsey, Mickey, Tawni, Shawni, and the rest of my teammates turn their heads toward me like sunflowers following the Sunny.

"Sorry," I mouth as I duck to slide onto the bench.

Coach Tina stops and gives me a hard stare. "Out of respect for your teammates and me, let's try to be more punctual next time, understood?" she says with her arms folded.

My face feels like it's on fire. "Yes, Coach," I reply, hanging my head.

"Now that we're all here, I'd like for us to do a team-building activity," Coach says, heading over to the storage closet.

Bea touches my shoulder with hers. "You okay? Coach really let you have it, huh? You looked so scared, I was afraid you were going to poop your pants," she whispers.

"I almost did." I take in a deep breath through my teeth. "I'll tell you one thing: I'll definitely never be late to practice again."

She laughs. "Okay, good. Just checking."

Coach Tina returns with a tennis ball. "For this game,

I'm going to need some help." She calls on the first two to volunteer, which happen to be Tawni and Shawni, the twins. "In a moment, both of you are going to go outside, and when you're called back in, your task will be to find this ball, which will be hidden somewhere in the gym." She takes a neon-green tennis ball and bounces it on the ground. "Whoever does it faster wins. Easy enough, right?"

Tawni shrugs. "Sure. Nothing to it."

Shawni throws her a playful glance. "You're going down, sister."

"You wish—I'm going to beat you so badly, you're going to wish you stayed in the womb." Tawni palms her in the face and Shawni whacks her arm away as they exit the room.

Coach explains further. "Here's where we come in. When Tawni returns, I want you to shout only positive words, like 'Great job' or 'You're doing awesome,' but you can't direct or correct her in any way. No hints or clues. Capisce?"

"Capisce!" we shout back.

Coach Tina runs over and tucks the ball in a little

crook behind the basketball hoop stand and goes to get Tawni.

She enters and the rest of the time plays out like a chaotic game of Hot and Cold, except we can't even say *cold*. When she heads closer to the hidden ball, we all cheer and yell, "Good job, Tawni! Yes! You got it!" but once she turns the wrong way, we fall silent. It takes her a good while until she finally finds the ball.

"Four minutes and twelve seconds." Coach Tina resets her stopwatch.

Tawni clasps her hands together and swings them from side to side like a champ. "Let's see if Shawni can beat that!"

Coach adjusts her visor. "All right, this time we're going to change it up. For Shawni, you can give whatever hints and clues you want as long as you don't give away the location of the ball."

"Wait a minute, now. That's not fair," Tawni interrupts, but Coach makes a zipping motion on her lips and she shuts up.

With a skip in her step, Shawni comes bounding into the room, and immediately someone yells, "Go that way!" pointing to the far side where the basketball hoop is.

Lindsey interjects, "Not that far, back up about two feet; you got it. A little more," until Shawni's standing a mere foot away from the hiding spot, but because of the angle, she still can't see the ball.

Mickey yells, "There you go. A little past your knee there. You have to crouch."

Shawni looks down and triumphantly pulls out the tennis ball.

Coach Tina lets out a low whistle as she clamps her fingers to stop her stopwatch. "Just under forty seconds. You win, Shawni!"

"In your face, Tawni!" Shawni does a celebratory series of cartwheels back to her seat as we cheer her on.

"Whatever—the game was rigged." Tawni scoffs, looking miffed.

"Now, Dollies. Let's talk about this 'rigging,'" Coach says. "Why do you suppose there was such a difference between how long it took Tawni to find the ball versus how long it took Shawni?"

"Well, it's pretty obvious. Tawni didn't get nearly as much help as Shawni," Bea says, rubbing her chin. "When Shawni went the wrong way, we were able to point her in the right direction."

Coach Tina looks around. "So let me ask you: Which type of feedback was more powerful? The kind we gave to Tawni, or the kind we gave to Shawni?"

We all point to Shawni.

"That's right, Dollies. The purpose of today's game was for you to see how much our performance can improve when we give and get specific and critical feedback versus just telling people what they want to hear," Coach Tina says. "Sometimes we think we're doing people a favor by agreeing with them or giving them compliments, but the truth is that people do better when they hear authentic critique." She bounces the tennis ball on the ground. "Sure, it doesn't always feel good to hear when we've messed up or hear suggestions for what we have to improve, but it does help us grow in the end.

"I want you to keep that in mind as we move into learning our new choreography. On this team, I want for us to talk to each other straight. When someone misses the mark, we should be able to call it out. Not because we're trying to be hurtful or to cut them down, but because we want the best for our team. That's how we become champions, by demanding it from each other, because every single person in this room is capable.

"Trust me, you wouldn't be here if you weren't. If we keep sharpening each other in the spirit of competition, there's nothing we can't do together," Coach Tina says, pumping her arm with conviction. "With that, I'm going to turn the rest of practice over to Lindsey."

For the remaining time, Lindsey shows us the first part of the choreography, and the routine is amazing. It's so original, I don't know exactly what genre it'd fall under: It's a little jazz, pom, and even hip-hop. She's got fouetté turns, straddle leaps, pirouette arabesques. Legit advanced dance techniques! But the showstopper is the two-person acrobatic solo Tawni and Shawni do for the finale. We should clean up with high marks if they can pull it off.

I'm so engrossed in practicing my combos, I don't hear Coach Tina approach from behind me. "Can I speak to you for a minute?"

"Sure," I squeak, nearly falling over in surprise. Knees shaking, I follow her back to the benches behind where everyone else is dancing. "What can I do for you, Coach?" I ask with a tremor in my voice.

She pokes her pen behind her ear. "Listen, I know I was hard on you earlier about being late, and I just want you to understand it's because I want more out of you."

I nod solemnly, feeling terrible for letting her down.

"It's clear that you're a shy one, and I'm fine with that. No one is saying you have to be a chatterbox, but I don't want you to fade away into the background either. I want you to understand that when you're late, it affects all of us, because you're an important part of this team. Like I said earlier, it's not just about being agreeable, it's also about contributing, being present, and also making this a priority. Do you understand what I mean?"

"I think so," I whisper.

She looks me directly in the eye. "Good, because I see a leader in you, Sunny."

I step back, rubbing my hands on my shorts. "Really? Me?" I literally haven't been called that since I was the line leader in kindergarten and everyone in the class got to be it at least once.

"Yes, absolutely," she says. "I could tell from the first time I saw you dance at tryouts. You notice things, you catch on fast, and I can tell that you've got a lot of really valuable insight that can make our team stronger, but that's not going to happen if it all stays locked up in your noggin," she says, pointing to her head. "I want you to work on that this season, opening up and being more authentic with yourself and others. You've got a lot to offer. I don't want you to worry about being a people pleaser here. Got it?"

"Yes, Coach," I say, brushing a sweaty tendril of hair from my face.

"All right, then—you can go back now," she says.

For the remainder of practice, Coach Tina's words

dig deeper and deeper into my brain. I've never really thought being a people pleaser was a bad thing, but she's not wrong; I often get so concerned about people's feelings and what they'll think of me that I end up keeping most of my thoughts to myself. But knowing that she thinks what I have to say is worth hearing makes me feel a tiny bit bolder, at least here, anyway.

✧ Chapter 18 ✧

When Bea and Jadyn first see my room, it feels almost like a show-and-tell session.

Bea picks up the snow globe from my dresser. "Sunny, is that you?" She shakes it so the glitter and metallic star confetti swirl around the tiny ballerina silhouette in the middle.

My cheeks warm. "Yeah, my parents got that made for me for Christmas last year. They used a photo from one of my recitals." I know it's supposed to be for little kids, but I still love it.

"That's so cool. I didn't know you do ballet, though it seems really obvious now. You move like a ballerina," Jadyn says, stretching his arms overhead into a classic fifth-position pose. "I did a bit, too, when I was little."

"Actually, I don't do ballet anymore." I bite my lip. "I quit almost a year ago."

"Really?" Bea asks, putting the snow globe back.

She points out all the ballet slipper knickknacks on my dresser. “From the looks of it, you were really into it.”

I shrug, feeling instantly regretful. “I don’t know. Maybe I should have kept at it.”

Jadyn takes the frame from my desk. In it, there’s a picture of me and Bailey dressed up as jars of peanut butter and jelly a few Halloweens ago. “Hey, I recognize this girl. Her name’s Bailey, right? She’s got social studies right after me. We sit in the same seat.”

“Let me see!” Bea says, coming over for a look. “Oh yeah, I’ve seen her around. She’s the one with the dark eyeliner, right?”

“Yup.” I nod. “She’s my best friend.”

“That’s hard to believe.” Jadyn’s eyes nearly bug out of his head. “No disrespect, but you two don’t seem like you’d have anything in common!”

“Why is that?” I ask, curious.

Jadyn shakes his head slowly like he’s not quite sure how to explain it. “Doesn’t she wear a shirt that has I HATE PEOPLE written on it?”

I burst into laughter. “Yeah, it’s her favorite.” I remember when she got it silkscreened in the kiosk at the mall. "Her sense of humor is on the snarky side."

"She sounds like fun." Bea elbows my arm lightly. "You should invite her over so we can all hang out sometime."

The mere suggestion makes the hairs on my arms stand up straight. Bailey is not shy about showing her true feelings about someone. Just ask Darren. Who knows what she'd say to their faces if given the chance?

"Uh, maybe . . . Yeah, maybe I'll ask her . . ." Sweat prickles under my armpits. "Are you ready to talk business?"

"Let's do it!" Bea shuffles through her notes from the last meeting. "Any news from the carpet shampoo lady on Greg's List?"

"Yes." Jadyn sits on the floor. "She got back to me and she wants to book us for Friday after school at four. Does that work?"

"Yup! Count me in," Bea says, jotting it down in her notebook. "Sunny?"

"Me too." The more group fundraising we do, the less I have to do on my own.

"Great, then I'll confirm with Mrs. Jones. That's her name, by the way. Also, Sunny, you'll be relieved to know that I told her how old we are and she said she's fine with it."

I let out a reassured sigh. It would have been beyond awkward dealing with that face-to-face.

"Also, I think I may have found us another gig, and this one pays a lot," Jadyn says, rubbing two fingers against his thumb.

"What is it?" Bea asks, all ears.

He reaches for his phone and shows us a picture of what looks like some kind of outdoor concert. "Well, while I was at the mall with my auntie this weekend, I saw that they set up a stage for local acts to perform for tips!"

"That sounds fun," I say. My cousin Yumi does something like that at her parents' Korean barbecue restaurant on weekends. Apparently, it's become such a big hit that they have to limit the number of people at the door. They're even thinking about opening a second location.

"When I went, there was a guy playing guitar and

singing a country song. He had the cowboy boots and hat and everything," Jadyn says, his eyes dancing. "I'm not kidding, people were throwing all kinds of cash into his tip jar! There had to be over a hundred dollars in there! Just for singing one song. Do you know how many songs I've sung for free in my lifetime?"

"A hundred dollars?" Bea repeats, her mouth gaping open like a fish's.

Jadyn sweeps his long legs into a crisscross-applesauce pose. "Yup, I looked into it and found out that they have a slot that's open next Saturday."

"There's no fee or anything to go on?" Bea asks, incredulous.

"Nope!" Jadyn says, giving us high fives. "It's free-ninety-nine."

"What would we perform, though?" I ask. Unease builds like Tetris bricks inside of me. "Because I can't really sing." On key, that is.

"We don't have to sing. We can perform anything we want. Dance, even." Jadyn gets up and starts busting a move. Suddenly, he gasps, and it's like a light bulb turns on above his head. "Should we choreograph something to a Supreme Beat song? Maybe 'Precious'?"

Bea and I start shrieking excitedly.

Within minutes, we've got the song cued up and we're buzzing with ideas for choreography.

The next hour flies by as we come up with the routine. Jadyn begs us to incorporate the sprinkler dance, and Bea insists on adding in some robot moves. I suggest some relevés and pliés from ballet. By the end of it, the dance is a chaotic mishmash of all three of our styles. It's goofy and playful and chaotic, but in the best way possible.

"Do you think it's okay to perform this in front of people?" I ask as I watch the playback of our super-kooky dance.

"Trust me," Jadyn says. "The more original it is, the better. It wasn't the flawless acts that were making the money, it was the fun ones. And this, my friend, is as fun as it gets."

"I think we can make this even more over the top," Bea says, stretching her neck to the side, making a cracking sound. "Maybe we can wear zany costumes or makeup or something?"

"All right, I have an idea that might sound a little random . . ." I start to say.

"What is it?" Jadyn asks.

I shake my head. "Actually, never mind—it would be too weird."

"Weird? That's exactly what we want, weird!" Bea says, leaning closer.

Jadyn rubs his hands together. "Now I really want to know."

"How about if we performed this dance . . . in inflatable dinosaur costumes?" I whisper.

Jadyn and Bea's eyes bulge like they've seen a dead body.

"Never mind. I knew it'd be too weird. I just suggested it because I already have one. . . ." I say, my cheeks burning bright red. "Forget I said anything."

"What? Are you kidding me? It's the best idea I've ever heard!" Jadyn says, jumping up and down.

"We have to do it," Bea says, pulling out her phone. "I've got some store credit at Costume City. I'm going to order one of those right now."

Jadyn's already texting someone. "If I'm not mistaken, I think my cousin has one from last Halloween." His phone dings with a reply. "Yup, we're in business! He said I can borrow it."

I look up. "We're really doing this?"

"Yes, we are," Jadyn says. "We have to. It's so us."

They're actually on board with my idea! They don't think it's immature or corny at all—in fact, they like it! "Okay, yeah! Let's do it!"

Right about then, Halmoni appears in the doorway. "I made Korean fried chicken. Come eat." She waves her hand so we'll follow her.

"You don't have to ask me twice!" Jadyn says, trotting close behind, pumping his fists in the air with joy.

As I'm going down the stairs, I get a text.

> **Bailey:** You want to hang out? My parents are fighting again and I need to get out of here. Can I come over?

Ack, I can't say no to that. Besides, the last two

times she's asked to hang out this week, I had to say no because of dance stuff. If I tell her I'm busy again, she might get mad.

> **Me:** Sure, how about it half an hour? I'm out running errands right now.

A little white lie never hurt anybody. Thirty minutes should be enough time to get Bea and Jadyn to leave before she gets here.

> **Bailey:** 👍

The tantalizing aroma of savory fried chicken hits our noses as we follow Halmoni to the kitchen, where she's got the whole spread ready: wings, spicy gochujang sauce, diced pickled mu, fried rice, and even French fries.

"Wow. That's a lot of food. . . ."

I should have known. It's my grandma's joy to feed people until they're in physical pain and can't move.

This could be a problem.

"I made it all from scratch, so eat a lot, okay?" She scoots the plates toward us.

"Yes, ma'am!" Jadyn takes a plate from the stack and helps himself to a hearty portion.

"It's like I've died and gone to heaven," Bea says before diving in herself.

I have to do something to move this along, or we could be here all night. "Pro tip: They're super spicy, so it's best to take huge bites like this." I shove a whole drumstick in my mouth and use my front teeth to scrape off the meat. If this doesn't make them eat faster, I don't know what will.

My mouth is totally full when Halmoni smacks my arm with a dish towel. "They will choke on it like that! Take small bites," she tells them, thwarting my efforts to speed up this meal.

"It's so spicy it burns, but in a good way," Bea says between dainty nibbles. "By the way, we can't thank you enough for being our chaperone for the concert."

Halmoni fumbles with the dishes. "Concert?"

I cough. "Sorry, I must have forgotten to mention it to you. Coach said we need an adult to take us to the concert while we're in San Francisco for the competition," I say, filling her in. "So I volunteered you, but don't worry—we're going to pay for your ticket. Just come and have a good time, okay?"

Halmoni looks uneasy as she wipes the counter. "I see. . . ."

Bea whispers, "Sunny, you haven't asked her until now?"

"I guess I just assumed . . ." I reply.

My grandma's eyes get soft. "I will try to go."

Try to go? What does she mean by *try to go*? This is Supreme Beat we're talking about. The band we've been obsessed with all year. What else could she be doing at that time that would be more important than them?

From a distance, I hear the garage rumble open.

Oh no, my parents are home early from work.

✧ Chapter 19 ✧

"Something smells good in here," Mom says, putting her purse down on a chair. She's wearing her work overalls and she's still got sawdust in her hair.

As if that wasn't embarrassing enough, Dad comes swooping into the room yelling "Sunny Bunny!" and buries me in kisses on the top of my head.

I pull away. "Dad, stop." Bailey teased me forever after she overheard my parents calling me that.

"Don't worry, my mom kisses me when she gets home, too," Jadyn says in a good-natured way that eases some of the humiliation. "But she leaves lipstick marks!"

"You must be Beatrice and Jadyn." Mom looks at them admiringly, like they're little golden treasures gifted from a faraway kingdom.

"In the flesh!" Jadyn wipes his saucy fingers on a napkin before extending his hand for a shake. "Your home is beautiful. Thank you for having us."

"We're so glad you're here," Mom says, shaking his hand. "It's been a long time since Sunny's had anyone over, other than Bailey."

My face reddens. She makes me sound like I'm such a pathetic loner, which I guess I am, but I don't need it advertised.

"How did your meeting go?" She squeezes my shoulder. "Did you come up with brilliant ways to earn money for the concert tickets?"

"For that Korean pop band?" Dad snaps his fingers like he's trying to remember something. "What's their name again? Supreme Sensation? These guys, right?" He busts out his very stiff and jerky rendition of their signature dance move, which regrettably includes a hip thrust.

My insides burn with shame. "Dad, please. Stop."

But then Jadyn starts clapping to cheer him on. "Mister Park! Mis-ter Park!"

Soon, Bea and Mom and even Halmoni join in the chant, which only makes Dad more emboldened with his dance moves. He flings his arms with so much flair that he accidentally bangs his elbow on the counter.

"Ouch!" He jumps up and down, cradling his arm in his hand. "Meant to do that!" he jokes, clearly loving all the attention.

What is going on?

I check my phone again. Eeek! Bailey will be here in just five minutes. Desperate times call for desperate measures. I need to get them out of here. Fast!

"Wow, is it really almost four thirty already?" I say, pretending to be surprised. "It's getting late, and I should probably get started on some homework soon."

Mom pulls a gallon of Häagen-Dazs ice cream from the freezer. "But we haven't even had dessert yet!" She flashes it in front of our faces temptingly. "It's coffee flavored. Your favorite, Sunny!"

Bea and Jadyn eye the carton longingly.

"Sorry, Mom, but I don't think we have enough time." I collect the dirty plates from the counter, and they clang as I stack them. "Mrs. Reyes will be here to pick them up any minute."

"Okay, we'll have to have you again another time and we can do ice cream then, I suppose," Mom says, putting the carton back in the freezer reluctantly.

"Here, I'll walk you guys out," I say, leading them down the hall.

"Bye, kids!" my parents say before I whisk Jadyn and Bea to the front door.

From down the hallway, I hear Mom ask Dad, "Is there something uncool about coffee ice cream?"

When we're outside, I whisper to my friends, "Sorry about that. It's just that my grandma gets cranky after a certain hour." I go with whatever comes to mind first. "Her meds and all." I rub my arms to warm them from the brisk evening chill as we walk down the driveway. "Sometimes my parents don't always remember her condition."

Jadyn nods with understanding. "I know what you mean. My granny, the one with the foster cats, she is a big grouch after she takes her pills, too. She says it makes her constipated."

I snort. "Thanks for understanding. I hope you didn't feel like I was kicking you out."

"Don't worry. You don't have to explain, Sunny," Bea says, waving her hand at me.

The bright glare of headlights floods the driveway as a car pulls up, but it's not Jadyn's mom's SUV.

It's a yellow Mini Cooper convertible.

My stomach shrivels into a hard knot as the door opens and a dark figure gets out of the car.

"Bailey! You're early. . . ." I hurry over to greet her.

Up until now, I've been doing everything humanly possible to avoid this moment—the collision of the friend groups—but here we are.

I just hope Bailey will be on her best behavior, but I'm afraid that might be asking for too much.

Bailey's got on a smug smile, like a cat waiting to pounce.

Gulp.

✧ Chapter 20 ✧

"You remember Jadyn and Bea. This is Bailey," I say, struggling to keep my voice steady as I introduce them.

"Yay, we finally meet!" Bea is bright eyed and eager to engage, without a clue that she's already been deemed irritating and immature in Bailey's *humble opinion*.

"Sunny has told us so much about you," Jadyn says, all teeth and sunshine.

"Is that right?" Bailey says, scrunching her nose like she doesn't quite believe him.

"Oh, definitely!" Bea pipes up. "She just showed us pictures of you in your peanut butter and jelly Halloween costumes when you were little."

Jadyn adds, "You two were so *precious*."

Out of nowhere, Bea busts out singing the chorus of the Supreme Beat song. "'P-p-p-p-precious, like a butterfly wing!'" Following her lead, Jadyn joins her, and pretty soon they're cracking up, belting out the lyrics while doing our dance choreo together.

I chuckle to myself. We've listened to this track so many times, the mere mention of the word *precious* will prompt a full-blown performance.

I glance over at Bailey, and she's not amused one bit. She's not even trying to hide it.

"Uhhh, okay," she says, her eyes narrowed and her voice dripping with disgust.

Oh no. My stomach turns somersaults.

"Don't mind us, Bailey. Just a little inside joke," Jadyn says, still chortling from their impromptu dance session.

"Apparently." Bailey presses her lips together so hard, they disappear.

I'm so uncomfortable, I wish the ground would open up and swallow us whole.

Thankfully, right then, a silver SUV pulls up on the curb and the window rolls down on the driver's side. Mrs. Reyes hangs her elbow out. "Did you have a good time, kiddos?"

"Hi, Mom," Jadyn says, jumping into the passenger seat.

"Before I forget. Here." Jadyn's mom reaches over and hands me an empty plastic container through the window. "Sunny, this is your grandma's. Please tell her I said that her dumplings were delicious!"

"You're welcome, and I will," I reply, tucking the Tupperware under my arm, acutely aware of the look of surprise on Bailey's face. Knowing her, she might feel some kind of way that Halmoni made dumplings for them, too.

"Thanks for having us!" Bea follows Jadyn into the car. "See you at practice, Sunny!"

Bailey's grin stops before it reaches her eyes.

As the car pulls out of view, I can almost feel myself shrinking next to Bailey.

We're walking inside together when Bailey snorts. "Jadyn and Bea are exactly how I expected them to be."

I slip off my shoes at the door. "What do you mean?"

She pauses. "How should I put this?" Her eyeballs dart upward as she searches for words. "I'm sure they're perfectly nice, in an innocent and childish kind of way, but they're a bit much, if you know what I mean." She gives me a challenging look that dares me to disagree.

"You think so? In what way?"

She snickers with a curled upper lip. "Oh c'mon, did you see how they were singing and dancing on your driveway? I was getting secondhand embarrassment just being there. Seriously, do they ever dial it down?"

"No, no, they're not always like that," I say, trying to deflect the barrage of negative vibes she's emitting. "They're really normal usually, especially when we're dancing. I don't know what got into them just now."

"If you say so." She clenches her teeth and inhales deeply. "I don't know what I'd do if my mom made me stay on the team with them."

I force out a chuckle. I swear, this lie is like the McDonald's McRib sandwich. Just when I forget it exists, it's back again.

She plants one hand heavy on my shoulder. "It must take a lot of patience. How do you do it?"

"I don't know. I just have to." Out of habit, I twist, making my torso crack, releasing the pressure from my joints. "They're my teammates. It's not like I have much of a choice." I don't even know why I said that. Maybe I felt bad about lying to Bailey. Or maybe I knew deep down that it was just the kind of thing she wanted to hear.

Bailey starts laughing gleefully. "Oh, Sunny, I'm so sorry. I shouldn't laugh at your situation!"

I give her a playful shove.

"So, what kind of errands did you have to run together, anyway?" She saunters toward my bed and rolls over onto her stomach so that she's facing me.

I look away. "We needed to pick up some supplies for uh . . . Coach Tina is having us . . . We're fundraising," My voice cracks as I scramble to come up with something that makes sense.

Her eyebrow arches. "Fundraising for the dance team? Is that a thing?" she asks with a twitch in her jaw.

My head bobs up and down so fast that everything is a blur. "Yup, the budget, you know. It's not a lot, and there were cuts. And, well, stuff is so expensive."

She sits up, giving me a hard stare. "What kind of stuff?"

My throat feels tight, like someone blasted me with a blowtorch. "Like the uniforms and other things, too. There're some new registration fees this year since the board changed. Super boring and complicated, but basically Coach wants everyone to raise money for the team. So we're doing odd jobs and things to make up the gap." Even I can hear how sketchy I sound.

She chews on her lip. "I've never heard of anyone on the dance team having to do that before."

"Yeah, I think we're the first team that's had to." Not wanting to get into this any further, I make my voice light. "Anyway, enough about dance stuff. What's the latest with Darren? Any updates?"

She lets out a barking laugh. "Ugh. You should see him these days." She sneers. "He got a new haircut and he's been going hard with this musky cologne, walking around with his head in the clouds, humming. He's basically advertising to the world that he's having an affair."

"Has your mom caught on yet?" I sit perched on the edge of my bed, my legs dangling from the side.

"No, she's been so busy at the juice bar, she hasn't noticed, but I'm going to tell her soon now that I have this." Bailey rustles around in her jacket pocket and pulls out her phone. "Check out what I caught him doing at lunch yesterday."

I'm a little afraid of what she'll show me, but it's like a car accident on the freeway—I can't not look.

She plays a video, but all it shows is Darren sitting at the kitchen table while her mom is making an avocado and alfalfa sprout sandwich. Then his phone rings, and he quickly gets up to take the call. The whole thing is fifteen seconds long.

"That's it?" I ask. This can't be the evidence she was referring to.

"Yeah," she answers, suddenly defensive. "Why?"

I hesitate. "Bailey, I don't know if this is enough proof that he's having an affair. He could be taking a work call for all we know."

She points to the screen. "Did you see the way he checked to see if my mom was watching him before he snuck off? He even shut the door! He's up to no good. The guilt is written all over his face."

"*I* see what you're saying, but I'm not sure your mom will," I say, careful not to minimize her feelings. "I think you're going to need more solid evidence to convince her. You know people don't want to believe what they don't want to believe, even if it's true. You need something she can't deny or explain away. Like a video where you can actually hear the other woman."

"You think so?" She's glum again. "I guess I'm back to square one, then."

I tap the video to watch it again. "I don't get it. How'd you get this footage if it was taken yesterday during lunchtime?" We were at school then.

"Oh, right." Bailey reaches into her pocket and pulls out a pen. "With this. I ordered it a while back. It's an app-enabled spy-cam pen," she explains, turning it to the side to show me. "See that black circle? That's the camera, and there's a microphone hidden there, too. I can stick it in my pocket or leave it wherever, and it'll record everything."

I inspect it close up. "I never knew there was such thing as a spy pen."

"Yup. I had to figure out how to get evidence without being obvious, so this was perfect. I left it on the kitchen counter at my mom's place when I went over last weekend."

I nearly fall off the bed. "You did? It's been there all week?" This level of privacy intrusion blows my mom's parade float spying out of the water.

"No, I only program it to turn on whenever I know Darren is over. The battery life isn't that good." She sighs. "I guess I've got to go plant it again. Maybe I'll leave it in the den this time. That's where he takes all his little calls."

Bailey glances up at me. "Actually, do you think you can help me? We can pretend to play hide-and-seek or something. That way it won't be suspicious that I'm snooping around in his man cave." She rolls her eyes.

"Yeah, sure. When?"

"I'm going shopping for bridesmaid dresses with my mom next Saturday. Want to come with us? We can plant it when we go back home to hang out."

Alarm bells sound in my head. Next Saturday? That's when Jadyn, Bea, and I are supposed to do our dance performance at the mall.

There's a prickle along the back of my neck. "Sorry, I can't."

Bailey's excitement fizzles instantly, and I'm back in hot water again. "Why not?"

"Uh, I've got this family thing my parents are making

me go to," I fib, tugging at a loose thread at the hem of my shirt and twirling it around my finger until it squeezes off my blood supply. I don't dare tell her it's because of dance again.

"Can't you tell them it's for a school project?" she says, unfazed. "I'm sure they'll understand."

"I wish I could, but . . . It's my cousin Yuri's birthday. . . ." I lie, biting my lip. As far as I'm aware, my cousin is still backpacking across Nepal with her new Peace Corps boyfriend, living her best life, but Bailey doesn't know that. "Everyone is going to be there. If I could get out of it, I would."

"Fine," she says flatly, examining her cuticles.

I can tell from her expression that it's anything but fine, but at least she lets it go for now. Hopefully it'll be one of those things that blows over by the morning.

Later that night, I log back onto the Fanverse chat, and everyone is talking about the upcoming concert.

I click around, and there's a new thread going of people who are trying to charter a bus together from a hotel. There's another group planning on meeting before the concert to trade photo cards. My body tingles with excitement.

I read on the message boards that the concert is only half of the experience. The other half is hanging out and getting to know other people in the fandom. I imagine being surrounded by fellow fans in cosplay and trading goodie bags full of swag. How fun would it be to participate in flash mobs, meetups, and all kinds of other fan events with Jadyn and Bea?

Maybe we can even perform our "Precious" dance! Or form a flash mob dance of our own!

Could we, though? Would it be too weird? I think Supreme Beat fans would get it, and it'd be a huge hit with them. . . .

I suppose I could just suggest it to Jadyn and Bea and see how it goes.

Right after I fire off my text, Halmoni pops her head in the door. "You're still awake?" she asks, already in her pajamas.

"Yeah," I tell her. "What's up?"

She gives me a funny look. "How can you sit like that?"

"This?" I laugh, noticing for the first time that I'm in

a pretzel stretch. "It's so comfortable!" It's an old dance habit. I sit up and scoot over to make room for her. "I'm catching up on Supreme Beat stuff. They just put up some new content. Do you want to watch with me?"

She shakes her head. "Ah, not tonight. I'm sleepy." The wrinkles in her face seem deeper today.

"You sure?" I pat the spot next to me to tempt her. "It's a funny one."

"You watch it. I'm going to bed early. I'll see you in the morning," she says before closing the door. "Good night."

"Night!" I call.

Halmoni has been turning in early a lot these days. I hope everything is okay with her. I get a niggling feeling that it's not, but at that moment, a text comes in.

Jadyn: Love the idea! Our Precious choreo is too good not to perform at the concert!

Bea: Yes, agree 💯. Should we do it with dino costumes or no?

Jadyn: YES TO THE COSTUME! DUH!

Jadyn: Also, don't forget, Mrs. Jones's house tomorrow for carpet cleaning at four. She's at 1700 Sycamore Lane. Don't be late, she sounds like she doesn't play around when I talked to her on the phone

Bea: Woop woop! Can't wait to clean some carpets and make some moolah! SB, here we come!

✧ Chapter 21 ✧

Jadyn was not wrong.

Mrs. Jones is a tiny old lady, but she looks like she wouldn't think twice about whacking someone across the knees with her cane if they tried any funny business with her.

"You're late." She eyes us sternly as she answers her front door.

My throat tightens, and I make sure to maintain a healthy distance between me and her cane.

"My apologies, Mrs. Jones," Bea says as we follow her down a dark hallway that's lined with a bunch of old family photos.

Her place reminds me of the Haunted Mansion ride at Disneyland. From the antique furniture to the china cabinet along the back wall to the faded floral wallpaper. Everything here probably has a bunch of untold stories behind it.

Bea adds, "We were walking all over the cul-de-sac, lost because we couldn't find your house number."

"The overgrown rosebushes are covering the porch, aren't they?" Mrs. Jones clucks her tongue with irritation. "I tell you, everything in this whole house is falling apart! The fence is sagging, the dishwasher only cleans on one side, and now the bushes need trimming. I can't keep up with it all. Ever since my husband passed, I've had to deal with one thing or another around here."

Jadyn frowns. "So sorry to hear about your husband."

"Nothing to feel sorry for. It was his time to go," she snaps, swinging open the door to the garage. "Mostly he was a pain in the rear, but now that he's gone, I realize just how much work he did around the house."

She switches on the light with a small sigh. "Bless his heart."

The first thing I notice are the power tools on the peg board above the workbench. I spot a DeWalt chop saw, an impact driver, a cordless orbital sander, and a high-end nail gun with air compressor. "Was this your husband's workbench?" I venture to ask. If my parents were here, they'd both be drooling.

"Sure was. Saul loved to fix things. Spent a fortune on his tools. And to think, they just sit there collecting dust now. Such a shame." She opens the storage cabinet and rolls out a huge tank-like contraption that you'd see in a history museum. "Anyway, here's the carpet cleaner.

"It's easy enough to operate. All you have to do is push it by the handle like you would a vacuum cleaner. You press down here to release the suds." She points out the lever on the side of the machine. "Do one pass to shampoo, then go back over it, and it'll suck it all back up. Leave it damp to air dry."

I take lots of mental notes. One thing is for sure: I do not want to mess up anything belonging to Mrs. Jones.

"Now, listen here." She holds up a spindly finger. "The only tricky thing is this little lever. It doesn't stay locked in place anymore, so when you want it to shut off, someone needs to pull on it or else the soap will keep coming out and make a big mess.

"Another thing, this machine is surprisingly heavy, so don't take your hands off the handle or it'll go rogue on you," Mrs. Jones warns.

"Don't you worry, we'll take care of everything," Jadyn

reassures her as she grabs her purse to head out. "Your house and your carpet are in very capable hands."

"We'll see about that." She pulls on a pair of giant sunglasses that make her look like a housefly. "I'll be back from my doctor's appointment in a couple of hours. If you need anything, just call my cellular."

"Sounds good, Mrs. Jones. We'll see you then," I say, seeing her off at the door.

It takes us a few runs before we get the hang of it, but soon we fall into a good rhythm. Bea is in charge of clearing the floor of furniture; I push the machine along the carpet while Jadyn holds down the broken lever with his hand, helping to keep it steady.

Nothing to it.

Meanwhile, Bea is catching us up on the latest on Taylor Tang. "I don't want to overanalyze, but we held eye contact for two whole seconds at the geology station in lab today. It wasn't very long, but I swear, I could feel the sparks—" All of a sudden, she stops midsentence.

She gasps, dropping to her knees in front of a hamster cage on the coffee table. "Mr. Pickles?"

"Who?" Jadyn and I say at the same time.

"This hamster is the spitting image of my old pet Mr. Pickles! He had the same black and white patches." Without hesitation, she opens the wire door and reaches to pull the hamster out.

"Bea, what on earth do you think you're doing? We do not have permission to do that!" Jadyn scolds. "Put that thing back right now!"

She ignores him. "Relax, I'm just going to hold him for a little bit. In memory of the late Mr. Pickles." She clasps the hamster in her hands and sticks her nose up to his. "Do you want to pet him? His fur is ridiculously soft."

His little whiskers wiggle when I touch his furry head. "Aw, he's so cute! You have to feel him, Jadyn!"

"Ew. Sorry, but rodents and I do not mix," he says, holding on to the carpet cleaner handle.

"How can you say that about this pwecious wittle thing?" Bea says in a baby voice, nuzzling him in the crook of her neck.

"Easy. It's the beady little eyes and the claws. They creep me out." Jadyn makes an exaggerated shivering motion. "Keep that Mr. Pickles incarnate far away from me, please."

"Suit yourself." Bea sits down and plays with the hamster. "Don't listen to meanie Jadyn over there. He just doesn't have an appreciation for cutie critters like yourself," she whispers loud enough for us to hear.

Jadyn and I get back to cleaning the carpet, and I'm feeling so proud of how straight and professional our vacuum lines are. We're about to start on the last part of the room when Bea jumps to her feet with horror in her eyes.

"Ouch! He bit me!" When she flips her hand around to see the bite mark, she loses her grip and accidentally tosses the hamster into the air.

Unfortunately, Mr. Pickles, or whatever his real name is, lands on Jadyn, who starts running around the room, screaming at the top of his lungs.

I run over to Jadyn, grab ahold of his shirt, and start fanning it wildly until the hamster is flung onto the floor.

Jadyn takes a deep breath. "That was the scariest moment of my life. Thank you for saving me, Sunny."

That's when I notice the soapsuds cascading from the carpet cleaner like it's Niagara Falls.

"Oh no!" I run over and yank the power cord from the outlet, but it's too late. The massive carpet cleaner has already crashed into the wall with a loud *thunk* before finally puttering off.

"Got him!" In one swift motion, Bea catapults her body to scoop the hamster up in her hand and puts him safely back into the cage, but the room is a total disaster.

"Are you okay, Sunny?" Jadyn comes toward us, kicking his way through the knee-high barricade of bubbles.

"Yeah, I'm fine," I say, inspecting the damage. "The soap should be easy to clean, but check out what we did to the wall." I step out of the way, revealing a huge softball-size gash.

Jadyn and Bea start freaking out. "What are we going to do? What do we tell Mrs. Jones? She's due back in twenty minutes!"

Feeling close to losing it myself, I take a deep breath and let it out slowly through my nose.

"I think I can fix this," I tell them, calmly channeling my inner Halmoni, who is always cool under pressure. "I just need some wire mesh and spackling paste. I'm sure Mrs. Jones's late husband had some in his workspace."

"Great, let's divide and conquer. You work on that while Bea and I clean up," Jadyn says.

After I gather the materials I need from the garage, I start scraping away the edges of the hole with a putty knife. Once it's smooth, I gingerly place the self-adhesive mesh over the circumference.

Jadyn and Bea get the soap situation under control surprisingly fast and come over just as I'm covering the patch with spackling.

"Wow, Sunny. How do you know how to do this?" Bea says, crouching, watching me work with open curiosity.

"Actually, I've never done this before, but my parents make parade floats for a living, so I'm pretty good with tools. I'm just going with my gut here." I feather the edges of the spackle so it blends with the wall's texture. "How does it look?"

"Incredible." Jadyn runs his hand lightly over the patch. "It's still damp, but you can hardly tell there was ever a hole. You're amazing!" he says, giving me a high five.

"Thanks," I say, blushing just a little. Who would have thought my handy skills would come in . . . handy?

Right then, we hear the front door creak open.

"She's back!" Bea whispers, a look of terror on her face. "Just be cool. We got this."

With no time to lose, I have no choice but to stash the bucket of spackle and other tools behind the couch just before Mrs. Jones joins us in the living room.

"Well, I have to hand it to you kids, the carpet looks fantastic!" She beams, inspecting our work.

"We're so glad you like it," Bea says, subtly scooting the putty knife under the coffee table with the toe of her sneaker.

"Well done, kids." Mrs. Jones gets out her wallet and hands us our payment of two hundred dollars. "Home feels a little more like home now, thanks to you three."

Relief rolls off my shoulders. "If you ever need help with anything else, please give us a call," I tell her, shocked that we're really pulling this off.

"I will, sweetheart," she says, but then she stops.

"Wait a minute." My body tenses up as she draws near to inspect the newly patched hole in the wall. She bends over to touch the surface, and her fingertips are white with fresh spackle. "There was a hole here when I left."

My heart stops in my chest. "A hole?"

"Yes, from the time my husband banged into it with a golf club. What happened to it?"

Shoot.

Jadyn, Bea, and I meet eyes. Obviously, the last thing I want to do is confess to Mrs. Jones how we messed up, but I know it's the right thing to do.

Gathering my courage, I squeeze my hands into fists in my pockets. "I'm sorry, it was my fault. It all started when we lost control of the carpet cleaner and it hit the wall. I thought we made the hole, so I patched it up for you. I didn't mean any harm. If you want, I can take it off for you, to keep your husband's memory alive," I offer, tugging at the corner of the mesh wire with my fingertips.

She starts chuckling. "That won't be necessary. Please leave it the way it is."

I look up. "So you're not mad?"

"No. Why would I be mad? I got my carpet cleaned,

and now my wall got fixed for free!" she says, waving her hand.

Jadyn, Bea, and I let out a collective breath of relief.

"I just wish you had told me about it on your own." Mrs. Jones clomps her cane on the ground for emphasis. "Kids, listen to me. It's okay to mess up, but it's not okay to pretend you did no damage." She clears her throat. "Whether you intended it or not, damage is still damage."

"We're sorry, Mrs. Jones. We should have said something to you," Bea says, her head lowered.

"You live and learn." Mrs. Jones points to me. "But now that I know you're good at fixing things, I'm going to have to hire you to help me with all my home projects around here. If you'd be willing, that is."

"I'd love that," I say sheepishly.

"All right, then. I'll see you starting next week," she says with a nod. "And before you go, make sure you put all that stuff behind the couch and under coffee table back where it belongs."

And that's the completely random way I got my job as Mrs. Jones's personal handygirl. Because of her, I have a real chance of earning the money I need for my concert tickets.

Who could have seen that coming?

Turns out, this wouldn't be the only surprising thing to happen to me this week.

✧ Chapter 22 ✧

Every day between second and third period, I meet Jadyn, who has the same nutrition break as me, at the picnic benches to swap snacks. It started off casually, but now it's become a thing. Once we realized that we're both foodies who aren't afraid to try new flavors, we made a point of bringing the most interesting foods from our pantries to trade. I've introduced him to Korean honey butter chips, wasabi peas, and Banana Kicks. In turn, he's let me try ube wafers, dried mango with chili-lime seasoning, and ham-and-cheese curls. So far, everything has been excellent.

"What goodies do you have for us today?" Jadyn asks, pulling a bag from his backpack.

"Shrimp chips," I reply, handing him one.

He takes a nibble of the French fry–shaped stick. "Oh, nice! It has a crunchy, light, airy texture, and it's salty but also a bit sweet and not excessively shrimpy!"

He claps his hands loudly. "Ten out of ten."

"Are those eggrolls?" I ask, looking at the bag in his hand. "Please say yes." I never met an eggroll I didn't like.

"Kind of. They're lumpia. My lola was in town and she made a huge tray. This one has ground pork in it, my favorite." He pops one into his mouth. "What is it with grandmas and why are their foods always so good?"

I take a bite. "Mmm, you weren't kidding! I could eat these all day!" Unfortunately, as I move to take another bite, my greasy lumpia slips from my hand and lands on the grass. "Oops. Got a little too excited there."

When I bend down to pick it up, Jadyn grabs my arm. "Sunny!" His eyes are wide with shock.

"What's wrong?" I ask, suddenly concerned.

Looking from side to side, he scans the quad like he's a secret agent. "You have to come with me. Quick," he whispers as he stashes the snacks in his backpack.

"What's the matter?" I say, following him down the side walkway. "Why are you acting so weird all of a sudden?"

"I'll explain in just a minute," he says as I trot behind him.

Now he's practically running through the halls, and I'm panting as I try to keep up with him.

Finally, he stops when we get to the empty library, and he opens the door.

"Jadyn, can you please tell me what is going on?" I follow him into the dark corridor near the back of the library, still winded and confused by our wild-goose chase through campus.

He puts his hand on my arm gently. "Sunny, I think you might have started your period," he tells me calmly.

Heat shoots up the back of my neck. "What? How do you know?"

"I have four sisters, remember? And, uh . . . your . . . pants . . ." He blanches and points behind me.

Scared, I turn to look, and there's an unmistakable splotch of red along the middle seam of my jeans. "Oh no!" I gasp, tears springing to my eyes.

Suddenly, everything feels like it's in slow motion. How am I getting my very first period in front of a boy, of all people? The sound of my blood pumping surges in my ears, and my hands start trembling. I'm hot and sweaty, and there's a sharp pain in my chest like I'm having a panic attack.

"It's okay. You're fine, Sunny. I'm going to help." Jadyn's soothing voice pierces my thick cloud of anxiety. He holds open the door to the bathroom. "That's why I brought you here, because there's a single stall so you can lock the door for privacy."

I'm crying now; the humiliation is overwhelming.

I can't believe this is happening. Bailey and I have been preparing for this since the beginning of the summer. She walked me through everything about Maxi Pads, period underwear, and even tampons, but all that stuff is sitting in the bottom drawer of my dresser at home, because that's where I assumed I'd be for my first period. Not here. Not now.

My breath catches in my throat. "What am I supposed to do about my pants?" I say between sniffles.

Jadyn digs around his backpack. "Here," he says, handing me a Tide stain-removing pen. "Use this."

I take it from him. "Jadyn, why do you have this in your backpack?"

"Well, I had a bit of an incident during the first week of school." He takes a deep breath. "Basically, Brenden Sylvester thought it'd be really funny to squirt barbecue sauce all over my shirt one day at lunch. I was so traumatized that now I never leave home without one," he says with an eye roll. "What a jerk."

"That's terrible!" Brenden Sylvester is a typical bully who loves to torture people just to watch them squirm. Everyone hates him but laughs along anyway because they're afraid of being his next victim. "I didn't know he picked on you."

"Constantly. How do you think I know my way around the library so well?" he retorts, raw emotion still lacing his words. "Until I started eating lunch with Bea, I used to hide out here so I wouldn't have to deal with him and his little minions."

My jaw drops. Jadyn is such a positive and perky person. I never would have guessed he went through all that.

"Yeah, but that's in the past. Thankfully." He sighs. "Anyway, see what you can do about getting the stain out and, I'll try to get you a pad from the nurse."

I check the time. "But the bell is going to ring soon! You'll be late for class. . . ."

"It's fine. I'll tell Ms. Arroyo the same thing I told Ms. Caputo when I was washing the barbecue sauce from my shirt," he says with a smirk.

"And what was that?"

"That I had diarrhea." He starts laughing. "Worked like a charm. She didn't even question me about it. Trust me, it's a fail-proof conversation ender."

I laugh, too. "You're a genius."

After he leaves, I clean up and line my underwear with enough toilet paper to stuff a mattress, then scrub my jeans with the stain pen until I'm able to get most of the blood out. It still looks like I wet my pants, but at least it's no longer red.

There's a knock at the door. "It's me, Jadyn."

Quickly, I put my jeans back up and wash my hands before opening the door.

He hands me a Maxi Pad and a hoodie. "What's this for?" I ask, holding up the official Ranchito Mesa spirit-wear sweatshirt

"I borrowed it from the lost and found. I thought you

could tie it around your waist until you get home. If you wash it and return it tomorrow, no one will even notice."

"Thank you!" I give Jadyn a huge hug. "You really saved me today."

"I know you'd do the same for me if the tables were turned," he says with a wave of his hand. "Not that it's physically possible, but you know what I mean."

For the rest of the day, it doesn't escape me that thanks to Jadyn I was able to dodge what could easily have been the most embarrassing day of my life. But, if I have to be completely honest with myself, a small part of me feels regretful that I shared this moment with him and not Bailey. Not that I could help it, obviously, but still, I wonder if this is yet another thing that'd make her feel left out if I told her.

Ugh.

✧ Chapter 23 ✧

Ever since I started working for Mrs. Jones, my goal of earning seven hundred dollars seems within reach. Somehow, I've already earned two hundred and ten dollars, and I'm motivated to do whatever I have to do to make this concert happen. If someone had told me that "making this happen" would involve standing on a portable stage in the mall's crowded outdoor pavilion, waiting to perform a K-pop dance in an inflatable dinosaur costume with my friends on a Saturday afternoon, I'd have laughed in their face.

But here I am.

My heart races as I squeeze into the line where the other acts are also waiting, which includes the same country music singer Jadyn saw a couple weeks ago, a few kindergarteners clad in sequin leotards and holding sparkly batons, and an all-female mariachi band.

"Are you doing okay in there?" I ask Jadyn, who is

dabbing his forehead with a hand towel.

"No one said anything about how hot it is in one of these things! I feel like I'm living inside someone's burp," he responds, his voice a touch irate as he zips himself inside his suit.

My nose wrinkles. Sometimes his descriptions are a little too spot-on.

"No whining allowed, Jadyn," says Bea from inside her costume. "Remember, we're doing this for Supreme Beat."

Butterflies flutter around in my stomach. "Just think, in a few weeks we could be seeing them from front-row seats!"

"Eyes on the prize, Reyes," I hear him muttering from inside his costume. "Eyes on the prize."

Right then, the emcee comes up to the mic. "Now, put your hands together for our next act! Let's give a warm welcome to the"—he stops to glance down at the cue card in his hand—"the Supreme Three Dance Troupe!"

Bea jumps with giddiness. "It's our turn!"

"Let's go!" Jadyn shouts, toddling in front to lead the way.

As we climb the steps to the stage, my insides clench, but there's a roar of laughter and cheers the moment we step up on stage.

I don't understand. We haven't even started dancing yet.

It dawns on me that they don't see us—they just see three goofy T-rexes.

The anonymity gives me a huge burst of courage, the same way it did when I did the dance challenge in my bedroom a month ago.

I've got this.

The first few bars of "Precious" hit, and I let loose.

We're lined up, swishing our hips and bouncing in and out of formation, moving in sync to the thundering beat, and the people are loving it!

I don't know if Bea and Jadyn are feeling the same electricity or what, but they're hitting their moves harder and crisper, too. The audience starts clapping and bobbing their heads along with the beat. Feeding off the energy of the music pulsing in my ears, I find myself stomping and strutting around the stage with unshakable confidence.

The crowd eats it up!

The cheers get louder as the beat drops, and we transition into our dance break, which is the part where our routine gets a little wacky. Thankfully, people go along with it. They scream as we bust out the robot moves and the sprinkler and the random ballet twirls. I can't help but notice a steady flow of people coming by to drop money into our tip jar, and it's filling up fast.

I can't believe that it's working! We're killing it!

I'm dancing my heart out, shaking and body-rolling with everything I've got, when all of a sudden, something catches my eye.

Did I imagine it, or is that Bailey and her mom walking past the food court?

My blood turns cold.

It is. What are they doing here?

That's right, they're bridesmaid dress shopping. Of course they'd stop at the mall! Why hadn't I considered that before?

If Bailey figures out that I lied about being at family thing in LA to be here, she's going to be royally pissed.

To my horror, they start walking toward us.

I keep dancing, desperately hoping she won't figure out it's me. But she literally saw me dancing to K-pop in this very costume a few weeks ago. It wouldn't take much for her to connect the dots.

The music is still going and our dance is not done, but I'm so stricken with fear that I make a break for it, and before I know what I'm doing, I'm sprinting off the stage as fast as I can.

With my heart beating through my chest, I crouch in the back area that's hidden from the view of the audience and unzip myself out of the costume, panting.

Overwhelmed, I force myself to breathe in. I breathe out until I feel like I'm in control of my body again.

I shouldn't have stranded Jadyn and Bea up on stage like that, but I didn't know what else to do. If Bailey found out the truth, that'd be the end of our friendship as we know it.

I hear the final note of the song, and Bea and Jadyn come running back to where I am, ripping out of their costumes.

"Sunny? Are you okay?" Bea asks, running to my side.

I'm tongue-tied. "Sorry. I . . . uh . . . I wasn't feeling too well."

"You look like you've seen a ghost," she says, squeezing my arm.

Embarrassed, I shake my head. "I'm fine now. I'm sorry. Sometimes I get really nervous with stuff like this."

Jadyn kneels so that we're eye level. "What happened?"

I open my mouth to reply, but the words don't come out. How can I explain to them that I lied to my best friend about being here today because I can't handle her disapproval? That would make no sense at all.

Instead, I go with a version of the truth. "It's kind of complicated, but I have panic attacks sometimes when I'm stressed. My doctor says it's because of my social anxiety." I slump into a chair, feeling ashamed of myself.

"Oh no, I'm so sorry, Sunny," Jadyn says, patting my shoulder. "My cousin also has it, and he has a hard time with performances, too."

Shame burns in my stomach.

Bea leans her head on my shoulder. "We're your

friends, and we'll help you get through this."

"I appreciate it," I tell them, still unable to make eye contact. "Sorry I ruined the performance."

"Actually, I don't think you did. People thought your exit was part of the routine!" she tells me.

"Really?" I look up, bewildered.

"It was so random, but people were cheering and putting more money in the tip jar after you ran away. Maybe because we were doing ninja moves right before, they thought we were the bad guys?"

Bea grabs an envelope from her tote bag. "Believe it or not, we made almost three hundred dollars! The guy said it was more than any of the other groups so far."

Wait. What?

"I know, right? I was shocked, too! But then again, we were really killing it out there today," Jadyn says as he gives us high fives. "We should be very proud of ourselves."

But the last thing I feel is proud.

After Jadyn and Bea get picked up, I sit on a bench, waiting for my grandma to come get me. Deflated, I stick in my earbuds to zone out, but as hard as I try, I can't stop replaying in my mind what happened earlier.

Now that I think about it, it's highly unlikely that Bailey knew it was me dancing up there, and I probably overreacted by running off like that.

I close my eyes, thumping my palm on my forehead, desperately wishing it were possible to go back in time and do it over.

Why do I have to be such a skittish scaredy-cat? But really, I already know the answer. It's because of Bailey. If it had been anyone else walking by, I wouldn't have freaked out, not to that extent, at least.

I sigh so deeply, the dried leaves on the ground rustle.

I don't know why I care so much about what she thinks of me, but I do. I always have. For the longest time, I thought this was normal, but now that I'm making new friends, I'm starting to realize it's not.

Whenever Bailey says something mean about my music or about my dance team, it hurts, but I never say anything to her about it, so she thinks it's okay. If Jadyn or Bea ever teased me for the things I'm into, I wouldn't think twice about telling them to knock it off. Why is that?

The difference is Bailey gets mad at me when I disagree with her.

I can already hear her response in my head. She'd say something like *What? I'm just being honest!* or *What's the big deal? It's just my opinion.* Or, worse, she might turn it around on me and accuse me of not accepting her as she is. It wouldn't be surprising if she ignored me for a day or two after that to punish me.

So what's the point of confronting her, then?

It's better to just avoid these situations altogether. It's worked up until now, hasn't it? But this whole concert thing is proving to be another kind of beast. I'm starting to feel like I'm in over my head.

And it's not just Bailey, either. I thought that being friends with Jadyn and Bea, people who really get me, would free me from all of that drama, but now I'm lying to them, too. The lies keep multiplying like laboratory mice, and I don't know how to make it stop.

The only silver lining in this situation is that it'll all be over soon. The concert is just six weeks away, and I won't have to keep any secrets after that. I just have to hang on until then.

✧ Chapter 24 ✧

"Are you ready? How do you feel?" I ask my parents as they pack for their long-awaited pitch meeting with the float sponsors.

Clearly nervous, Dad scratches the back of his neck. "Well, the prototype looks fantastic and the tech is working great, so if they don't choose us, then at least I can genuinely say that we tried our best."

Mom halts from zipping her suitcase to give him the look of death. "We cannot go into this meeting with that attitude. We need to be confident. None of this *We tried our best* nonsense. I want you to believe that we will come out victorious!" she says like she's making a speech in the front line of a battle.

Dad laughs. "If you say so, honey."

Still shaking her head, Mom attaches her luggage tag to the handle. "Sunny, are you sure you're going to be okay without us? I know Las Vegas isn't that far away, but we'll be out of town for more than two weeks."

I sit with my knees tucked to my chest at the foot of their bed. "Don't worry, Mom. I'll be perfectly fine. And anyway, I'm not going to be by myself. Halmoni lives here now, remember?"

"Well, your grandma doesn't technically live here . . ." Dad clarifies, holding up his finger. This is the reason Mom is always teasing him for being a know-it-all: He can't resist butting into conversations with *Technically* . . . Mom says it's an engineer thing.

"Well, seeing as how she's been here for over a year and she gets her mail here, I think it's safe to say that she's living here now," I reply.

"Fair enough." He coughs into his fist. "Make sure you listen to her while we're away."

"You know I will. I always do." I bite my lip. "By the way, have either of you noticed anything strange about her lately?"

"What do you mean?" Mom asks, looking a little alarmed.

"I don't know. The past few days, she seems tired and preoccupied whenever I try to talk to her. Like she's got something on her mind or maybe she's got the blues again. And she's been on the phone a lot with Imo Halmoni, too." That's her sister in Korea who runs a dance academy. I met her once when I was little. She looks exactly like Halmoni, just taller and younger and with lots of gold teeth. "Is there something going on with her?"

Mom and Dad do that thing where they meet eyes and telepathically send each other messages that I don't understand.

"Maybe she's a little down because the anniversary of Grandpa's passing is coming up," Dad says, folding his socks into a little pile.

I think about it for a moment. "Oh." I didn't even consider that, but it does explain a lot.

His expression turns serious. "Sunny, you can be honest with us. Are you sure you're okay with us going away for so long?" He rubs his face, raking his fingers along his cheeks the way he does when he's edgy. "I know you've been stressed out about regionals and earning money for your concert tickets. I don't want to be gone while your anxiety is through the roof."

Oh brother. I wish Halmoni were here to back me up and tell them to stop coddling me.

"Dad, I'm not stressed at all. In fact, I'm totally fine. Regionals isn't for another month and Coach Tina says we're already acing it. And the fundraising part is going well, too. Not to brag, but I've already managed to line up a dozen jobs with Mrs. Jones, so I'm on track to earn the money I need for the tickets."

"You have? By yourself?" Mom asks, baffled. I can tell she's holding back. Normally, she'd have given me a giant bear hug and covered me in kisses by now.

"Yup." I wind my arms across my chest, proud of myself.

Dad lets out a low whistle, rubbing the stubble on his chin. "And here I thought we'd have to give you some odd jobs around the warehouse to help you out, but it looks like you've already got it under control."

"That's right." I put my arms around their shoulders. "So please, stop worrying about me and worry about how you're going to kick C&C's butt and bring home that Kiwanis contract for Parade Brigade instead!"

Later, I'm about to stop by my grandma's room to say good night, but when I get to her door, I hear her speaking muffled Korean on the other side. She must be on the phone with her sister again.

Not wanting to interrupt, I head back to my room, but I stop dead in my tracks when I hear her say my name.

"Sunny? No, no, I haven't told her yet," I catch her saying in Korean.

On impulse, I scamper back to the door and press my ear against it.

Concentrating hard, I try my best to wade through the Korean words I don't understand. I can only make out snippets of the conversation here and there.

"I hope she doesn't get too upset," she says in a worried tone.

A trickle of dread runs through me when I hear her say something about "telling her when it's a better time." There are lots of *aigos* and *eomeos*, which she only says when something bad happens.

When the conversation ends, I sneak back to my room, my head swirling with questions: What was

Halmoni saying? What news is she keeping from me? And why would I be upset?

It doesn't sound like she's talking about Grandpa's death anniversary. It sounds like something is wrong with her and she doesn't want me to find out!

Now that I think about it, she has been lying down a lot, and yesterday she skipped dinner, which is unusual. She said it was a nighttime-fasting thing for her diet, but maybe that's just a cover-up. The way she's acting reminds me of how she was when she first moved in after Grandpa died. I hope this doesn't mean she's depressed again. But what is there to be depressed about?

Is she sick? Is she depressed about being sick?

But that's impossible. She's as healthy as a beast. She can still beat me in arm wrestling, and she's always bragging about how she can out-dance the ladies in Zumba class. There's no way she's ill, is there?

Suddenly, I remember the norigae she gave me and how weird she was being about the concert.

I stop myself because I know that if I don't, I'll spiral into an endless loop of worst-case scenarios that will trigger my anxiety.

I breathe deeply through my nose and let it out slowly. There's nothing I can do about this now. I'll have to wait until Mom and Dad get back from their trip to ask them what's going on.

Exhausted, I throw myself onto my bed, landing on my old Hello Kitty stuffy. It's the one Mom bought me for my birthday. I didn't have the heart to tell her that I'm not into Sanrio characters anymore, because I didn't want her to feel bad. I hope that's not what Halmoni is doing to me right now.

For the rest of the night, I toss and turn, doing everything I can to stop thinking about my grandma and her phone conversation, but I can't seem to beat back the fear that if she sinks into that dark place again, she might not be able to come out of it this time.

That's it. Now more than ever, I have to get her to that concert. Supreme Beat was the thing that shook her from depression last time.

It's the only way.

✧ Chapter 25 ✧

"Wow, I can't believe how lucky I am," Bailey says flatly, her words dripping with sarcasm. "To think, Sunny Park, the Dolly extraordinaire, is actually making time for little ole me!" She sits in my tulip-shaped chair and kicks her feet up on my bed.

"C'mon, Bales, don't be like that," I tell her, my legs dangling from the side of my bed. "You know I don't make the dance team schedule; Coach Tina does."

Though that isn't the whole truth. Dance team practice is only once a week. The real reason I've been swamped is because I've been working my butt off either for Mrs. Jones or one of her neighbors almost every day after school. That little lady has been talking so big about my handy skills, I've been getting booked left and right, which I suppose is a good problem to have. Except now Bailey keeps guilt-tripping me about how I've been too busy for her.

She twists her hair into a bun and secures it with a band from my desk drawer. "I don't get it. Why do you have to practice that many times a week? It's not like you're going to the Olympics."

"I know, Coach Tina takes it way too seriously," I say with a short laugh. "It's like the dance team is her whole life." It's funny—this is something I've joked about with Jadyn and Bea a bunch of times, but it feels a lot meaner saying it here to Bailey.

She turns away with disdain. "I'm so glad I didn't make the team."

I nod emphatically. "Seriously, it's a good thing you didn't. I can't wait to get my life back when the season is over," I say with an eye roll.

It makes me gush with regret to say, but I know from experience that it's the only way to get her to move on to something else.

Bailey sighs deeply. "Anyway, can I tell you about my mom? She is being so ridiculous lately. You should see what she's making me wear at the wedding. It's the cheesiest dress I've ever seen in my life. Pepto Bismol pink with tulle and little rosette buttons!" She makes a fake-vomit sound. “It makes JoJo Siwa look edgy.”

“It’s only for one day, right?”

“I guess.” She sighs. “At least you’ll be there to help me endure the torture.”

“I wouldn’t miss it.” It’s been on the calendar since Mrs. Stern announced the wedding date. Mom is making Dad go, too, even though he hates getting dressed up. “August eighth, right?”

“Yup, otherwise known as the worst day of my life.” She pulls open another desk drawer and pokes around. “Don’t you have any gum or candy in here?”

But then she stops suddenly. “Sunny Park. What is this?”

A tightness in my chest forms when I see her holding up a note folded into a heart shape.

“Nothing! It’s nothing!” I lunge to snatch it from her, but she’s too fast.

“Is this what I think it is? Is this a loooooove letter?” she says with a singsong voice, prancing around my room. She stretches her arms and opens the note high above my head so I can’t reach.

"No, Bailey! It's not! I swear. Give it to me!" I jump, but I'm not tall enough to grab it from her.

She opens the note and starts reading. "'Dear Taylor.'" She pauses, a glint of mischief dancing in her eyes. "Wait, is this to Taylor *Tang*?"

"Stop!" I'm tugging at her arm, but she's just too strong.

She squints to read the loopy cursive handwriting. "'I think you're cute and we'd make a great couple. Love, Your Secret Admirer.'"

Desperate, I plead. "Please, Bailey. Just give it back."

Bailey purses her lips, clearly amused. "You have a crush on him and you never told me? Your own best friend?"

"For the last time, I don't have a crush on Taylor Tang!" Giving up, I slump onto the chair in a huff, annoyed that she's refusing to listen to me. "I've been trying to tell you, it's not from me! I only have it because I'm supposed to deliver it to him. If you don't believe me, look at the handwriting."

Bailey's eyes travel between me and the note and

back before she speaks. "Hmm, you're right. This is definitely not your handwriting." She inspects the note again. "Whose is it, then? Who is in love with Taylor Tang? You have to tell me." She tugs at my desk chair, rolling me next to her. "Sunny?"

I can't look her in the eye. "I promised not to say."

She gets in my face. "Okay, fine. You don't have to, but blink once if it's Jadyn Reyes. It is, isn't it?"

Shocked, I open my eyes wide to remove all doubt. "No, it's not Jadyn! Not at all!"

"Then it must be Bea Papadakis!" She searches my face for a reaction, like it's some kind of crystal ball that will confirm her suspicions.

"Uh, nope. Not her either!" I say, but my voice gets weirdly high-pitched.

"Sunny, who are you trying to fool?" she says, reading straight through my bluff. "I've been your best friend since third grade. I can tell when you're lying. It's Bea—it's written all over your face."

I bury my head in my hands. Why do I have to have the most un–poker face in the whole wide world?

Her eyes dart upward. "Now that I think about it, I've

seen her hovering around the boys' locker room after fourth-period PE, probably stalking Taylor!"

I don't say anything, because what can I say? That's exactly what Bea's been doing.

Bailey looks at me with faux sympathy. "Okay, but real talk: I don't think she has a chance with him. Taylor is one of the hottest guys in our grade, and she's . . . Well, she hasn't even developed yet. It's kind of cute and pathetic at the same time that she has a thing for him." She clenches her teeth to make an awkward face. "I wonder if Taylor knows. . . ."

My head pops back up. "You CANNOT tell! Bailey, promise me you won't say a word. She'd be mortified if this got out. She hasn't told anyone but me and Jadyn. You have to keep this between us. Please!"

She snickers, ignoring me. "But this is such juicy gossip!" She's enjoying this way too much.

I grab her arm. "Bailey, I'm serious. Don't tell."

She flings her arm, freeing herself from my grasp. "Calm down, Sunny. I'm just messing with you. My lips are sealed." She makes a motion of twisting a key over her mouth. "I promise."

I exhale.

Bailey is definitely one to stir up drama just for drama's sake, but in all the years I've known her, she's always been true to her word. I can trust her.

At least I think I can.

✧ Chapter 26 ✧

A few days later, Jadyn and I go over to Bea's after school to help her make party favors.

"Thanks for coming," she says, answering the door. "You two are lifesavers. When my aunt said she'd hire me to make slime for my cousin Lauren's birthday party, she conveniently left out that it was for fifty kids."

Jadyn grabs his head with both hands. "What the . . . Fifty kids! I don't even think I know fifty kids."

"Imagine the buttload of gifts she's going to get, though," I joke, taking a seat on the bench in her dining room, which has been converted into a makeshift slime factory.

"Right? My aunt is big on inviting everyone, and she's got this huge house, which is great, but she told me just today that they need to be ready by tomorrow." She empties all the materials from a cardboard box. "I love my aunt Lillian, but that's short notice! There's no way I would have been able to finish this myself."

"No worries, Bea, we got you." Jadyn turns his baseball cap backward, scoping out the glitters, essential oils, glue, contact lens solution, baking soda, and food-coloring bottles she has out.

"That's what friends are for." I flash her some finger hearts before sitting down on the opposite side of the table.

"You're the best." Then she proceeds to explain the assembly line of tasks and what we need to do. I get assigned to the glue and food-coloring stations, and we get to work.

"So, how are your jobs going this week? Have you been raking it in?" Bea mashes slime and lets it ooze through her clasped fingers.

"I'm doing all right, if I do say so myself," Jadyn says proudly, up to his elbows in sparkly slime. "I've been working at my mom's salon every day. I've also been mowing the lawns of almost every neighbor on the block. It's not glamorous, but it's adding up."

"That's awesome, Jadyn!" Bea says.

"How much money have you pulled in?" I dare to ask.

He checks his phone notes app. "So far, I've earned four hundred and eighty dollars."

"Almost there," I tell him. "What about you, Bea?"

"I'm doing okay. Babysitting is where the money's been for me. You'd be surprised how much my aunt Heidi is willing to pay to go on a date night away from her toddler. Right now, I'm at about four hundred, but it'll be four hundred twenty after this slime job."

"I have about the same," I add. It's technically four hundred forty dollars, but who's counting?

"Great job, Sunny!" Jadyn gives me a fist bump. "See, you were worried for no reason. Look at you, killing it over here with your handygirl services!"

I laugh. "It's not me. Mrs. Jones has been the one getting me all the jobs!" If I had to ask around for myself, I'd be dead broke.

"That's awesome! Sounds like we're all on the right track. We've still got five more weeks until the tickets go on sale. Should be plenty of time to earn the rest of the money at this rate."

Jadyn swirls the turquoise and pink colors together as Bea sprinkles a dash of tangerine fragrance into the bowl. "Don't you just love this texture?" he says. "It's so squishy. I could do this all day."

"Super satisfying, right?" Bea stretches out her sparkly lavender slime like she's pulling apart a grilled cheese sandwich.

"So, Bea, what's the newest with Taylor?" I ask, wiggling my eyebrows up and down.

Her shoulders slouch. "Not much, sadly." She digs her fingers deep into her slime. "Ever since you snuck my letter into his backpack, he's been ignoring me, and I don't know why!"

"That doesn't make any sense. You said he doesn't even know you were the one who sent it, right?" Jadyn says, his mouth bunched on one side in confusion.

"Yeah, but I swear he's been acting weird around me since that day. I can't figure it out because the only people who know about the letter are in this room." She shrugs helplessly. "Before, I used to 'bump into' him by the boys' locker room every day, but now he goes the other way to his class!" She throws her slime into the container. "I wish I knew what went wrong."

I gasp. Did Bailey tell him? She knew Bea liked to cross paths with him there at that very time, and now he's mysteriously taking a different route? Could this be a coincidence?

"Neither of you said anything to him about me, did you?" Bea asks.

"Nope, I haven't said a word." Jadyn holds up a firm hand.

"Me neither," I answer. My insides feel as gooey as the slime in my hands. Technically, I didn't, but I did tell Bailey, and if Bailey told anyone else, then it'd be the same as me blabbing Bea's secret. The thought that I might be ultimately responsible for Bea's fizzled crush makes me feel sick to my stomach, but Bailey wouldn't tell, would she?

"There are a million reasons why you haven't run into him. I wouldn't sweat it," Jadyn says, vigorously kneading the slime dough.

Bea sighs heavily. "Maybe."

Jadyn's probably right. Who knows why Taylor is going the long way? Maybe he got a new pedometer and wanted to get his steps in. Maybe he needs to stop by the bathroom on that side. There's no reason to jump to conclusions. Anyway, Bailey promised me she'd keep it a secret, and I have to trust that she did. I'm probably just being paranoid.

"Hey, Sunny. Any more news on your grandma?" Jadyn asks.

I look up as I pour the white glue from the gallon-size jug. "My grandma? You know, she's still strangely quiet, and I still feel like she's avoiding me, but I haven't seen her coughing or wheezing, if that's what you mean."

"That's good news," Bea says. "Do you think maybe things got lost in translation when you overheard her on the phone?"

"It's possible. My Korean isn't that great. Hopefully I've been freaking out over nothing." It wouldn't be the first time.

"That makes two of us." Bea lets out a breath. "But I'm glad to hear your grandma is looking healthy. I know you were pretty scared there."

"Yeah, my parents are always telling me not to

assume worst-case scenarios." I squeeze a few drops of lavender food coloring into my concoction. It's one of the things I'm working on with my therapist. "Thanks for asking."

Bea squirts some of the contact lens solution into the slime mixture. "That's what friends do for each other, right?"

"Right," I reply, massaging the mixture with both hands.

It's funny how you can go your whole life without realizing what you're missing if you've never had it. Like something as small as Bea asking about my grandma. In all the time that I've been friends with Bailey, I don't think she's ever asked me about my family or anything I might be worried about. Not that she doesn't care—I'm sure she does—but she's not the type to inquire, and I'm not the type to talk about it unless someone asks.

"Hey, Jadyn. Guess who I ran into at Starbucks yesterday?" Bea says, popping the top on a jar of slime.

Jadyn shrugs. "Who?"

"Brenden freaking Sylvester."

Jadyn rolls his eyes and groans at the mention of his

name. "Ugh, how unfortunate. I'm so sorry."

"Don't be. While he was walking to get his Frappuccino, I made sure to accidentally stick out my foot and trip him," Bea says with a sneaky grin.

I burst into laughter. "Bea!"

"For you, my friend," she says doing a fancy curtain-call curtsy.

"Bea Papadakis, you are too much!" Jadyn cackles. "Watch out, though, he might mistake all that attention for flirting."

At that, she fake barfs, tossing some slime so it looks like it's spewing out of her mouth. "Did it look real?"

"It totally did!" I laugh out loud. "Let me try!" I grab my slime and join in on the fun.

We're one-upping one another with our Oscar-worthy vomit performances when I hear a ding from my backpack.

I reach for my phone to find Bailey texting me.

Bailey: Sunny, I need you to come over

Me: Now? Sorry but I'm kind of busy right now

Bailey: What are you doing?

Me: Dance team stuff

Bailey: AGAIN?

Me: Yeah, sorry

Me: What's up?

Bailey: It's urgent, please

Bailey: I need you to come over RIGHT NOW

Me: OMG is everything ok?

Bailey: I'll explain when you get here.
COME ASAP

Me: I'll see what I can do

Bailey: Hurry

A bad feeling comes over me.

Is Bailey having another breakdown? Just like the day of tryouts?

There must be panic in my eyes, because both Jadyn

and Bea stop goofing around when they see my face.

"What's wrong? Is everything okay?" Bea asks, putting down her slime.

I try to block the gnawing sense of dread that something terrible is happening to Bailey. "I'm sorry, but I have to leave."

"Oh no, really? Now?" Bea's mouth turns down. "Is there some kind of emergency?"

I reread the texts. "I think so."

"What happened?" Jadyn asks gently.

"I don't know the details." I wipe my hands on a paper towel. "But Bailey just texted that she needs me to come over right now."

"Out of the blue? Did she say why?"

I shake my head. "She just said to come."

There's a pause.

"Wait, so you don't even know what's the matter and you're going to run out on us like that?" Jadyn asks with his hand fixed on his hips, looking miffed. "Why don't you call her and ask first?"

Bea takes a softer tone. "Are you sure you aren't

jumping to worst-case scenarios? Like what you were saying earlier about your grandma."

"You don't understand. She's been having a really rough time lately with her mom's wedding. She needs me."

Jadyn holds up his palms in surrender. "You gotta do what you gotta do."

I grab my gym bag from the floor and sling it over my shoulder. "I'm sorry, but I'll make it up to you," I say, rushing out the door. "I promise!"

✧ Chapter 27 ✧

I run into Bailey's room at a full sprint. "I'm here! Are you okay?" I ask, breathless from booking it five blocks to her house. "What's going on?"

"Sunny, hurry!" Bailey beckons me to her desk, where she's watching some kind of livestream on her computer. "It's footage from the spy pen! Darren's about to get caught!"

I gasp as I stoop to watch with her. The image quality is really pixelated and hard to make out, but the audio is crystal clear.

"She must be the woman he's been talking to!" Her finger trembles a little as she points to the slender twenty-something following Darren into the dark kitchen. She's wearing a crop top and patterned miniskirt, and her long hair cascades down to her back. "Gross, why is he bringing her to my mom's place? And why is she half his age?"

We both gasp when suddenly the lights come on.

A woman in an apron and hairnet walks in.

"It's your mom!" I shout.

Our jaws drop.

But then Bailey's mom does something that neither of us saw coming.

She reaches out and pulls the young woman into a bone-crushing hug.

"What is going on?" Bailey says, looking like she just got smacked across the face.

The woman speaks. "Jennifer, it's so great to finally meet you. Uncle Darren has told me everything about you."

We turn toward each other in shock.

"Uncle Darren?" Bailey repeats, still stunned. Livid, she shuts off her computer monitor and buries her face in her hands. "I didn't know he has a niece!" she wails.

"It's okay, Bailey. You had no way of knowing." I couch my words as tenderly as possible. "Even I was convinced something was going on between them."

Her eyes brim with tears that threaten to fall at any moment. "This means, if there's no affair, then there's nothing standing in the way of my mom and Darren getting married." The realization hits her like a ton of bricks. "This is going to happen, isn't it?" she says, bawling.

I put my arm around her and give her a firm squeeze.

"Whatever." She dries her eyes with her sleeves, and her face goes back to being unimpressed and composed, which honestly frightens me more.

"I'm sorry, Bailey." The last thing I want is for her feel dead inside, moping around and listening to sad songs.

I have to fix this. I'm the only one who can. There must be something I can say to break her out of this moment or she'll get stuck again, and who knows for how long?

"Bailey, guess who I am?" I ask, poking her shoulder. Before she can even answer, I make a series of high-pitched squawking sounds that's supposed to be Bea's laugh.

She cracks a smile. It worked, so I do it again, louder and more exaggerated this time, which makes her start laughing. Soon her eyes are moist and she's throwing her head back, making hiccupping sounds. I hate to do this, but it's the only thing that always makes her laugh, and she desperately needs a laugh right now.

"Why is that so funny?" she says when she finally catches her breath. She pulls me into a hug. "I really needed that, Sunny."

I nod knowingly.

"How'd you get here so fast, anyway?" she says, checking the time stamps on our texts. "I swear I just texted you a second ago, and before I knew it, you were here."

"I sprinted here from Bea's house!" I admit. "With all this dance practice, I've got really strong legs," I say, patting the muscles on my thigh jokingly.

"Did you really run all the way here? From Bea's house? For me?" She touches foreheads with me.

I nod.

She pulls me into a hug. "You're so ride-or-die. I knew I could count on you."

Later that night, I lie in bed and go over the events of the day as I always do. It was a blur, and so much happened, but I keep thinking about that thing Bailey says, how I'm so "ride-or-die."

In a way, it makes me feel good because she's

appreciating me, but lately it's been making me feel something else. It occurs to me that the only time she ever says that about me is after I give up something big for her. Like when I quit ballet, or when I thought I wasn't going to be on the dance team. And now she's saying that about me leaving my hangout with Jadyn and Bea? It seems unfair that I have to sacrifice something I love for her to see that I've been a true friend to her this whole time.

I never ask Bailey to forfeit things for me—why does she constantly ask it of me?

Suddenly hot with anger, I kick off my blankets.

Maybe being a ride-or-die friend isn't all it's cracked up to be.

✧ Chapter 28 ✧

With regionals around the corner, things are heating up on the dance team, and there's little time for anything else. We're still tightening up loose ends, but Coach Tina says that we are looking really good, and that's not a compliment she gives easily.

There's only one part of our routine that still makes me nervous, and I'm not even in it. It's the twins' acrobatic stunt in the grand finale. Not that I doubt they can execute it. They are amazingly talented gymnasts, after all, but if Shawni misses her mark by more than a few inches, she's stomping right on Tawni's head. I guess that's what makes this part of the choreography so captivating, the danger of it all.

Right on cue, the music softens as Tawni arches into a backward bend with her hands on the floor. Gracefully, she lowers herself until her body is lying flat.

Then the booming beat drops and Shawni launches

herself into a dramatic no-hands arial flip over her sister, landing on both feet, mere inches from her face.

My muscles go weak with relief as the music fades out, and Shawni strikes her ending pose.

My teammates and I burst into applause. If we're still this impressed after seeing it week after week, I can't even imagine how the judges will react.

"Bravo!" Coach Tina shouts, aggressively clapping. "I don't want to jinx it, but if we bring this level of dancing to regionals, I have no doubt that we can beat out the Mustangs for the title! Then it's hello, San Francisco for us!"

Lindsey starts cheering, and we all join in.

"Now, before we wrap up today's practice, I have something to give you." Coach Tina grabs a big box from the floor. "Gather around!"

Bea, Jadyn, and I exchange looks. "What could it be?" I ask.

"Your new performance uniforms!" she announces, ripping off the packing tape.

Excited squeals and applause bounce off the studio walls, and we start closing in on her like a pack of hungry wolves, desperate to sneak a peek at what's in the box.

"I've been waiting the whole season for this," Jadyn says as he jumps up and down to see over the horde of girls in front of us.

Bea closes her eyes like she's saying a prayer. "Please don't let it be too big. Please don't let it be too big."

"Here they are!" Coach Tina reaches into the box and holds up the most gorgeous sparkly navy-blue one-sleeve dress with an ombre silver bustle skirt. "What do you think?"

Everyone in the studio takes a collective deep breath before a medley of shouts break out: "It's so cute!" "Sweet!" "I love it!"

My stomach flutters. I can't believe *I* get to wear *that*!

"Where's mine?" Jadyn asks Coach Tina, looking a little out of sorts.

"Ah, of course!" She pulls a boy version with pants from a smaller box. As soon as she hands it to him, we all make a mad dash to the bathroom to put them on.

The moment I see my reflection in the studio mirrors, I'm speechless. It's stunning on its own, but seeing us all in the same uniform gets me a little choked up.

I still can't get over the fact that I belong to this group of hilarious, dedicated, and talented dancers. Before this, I was just a shy, self-doubting ballet dropout, and now I have a whole team of friends I get to compete with. In these cute uniforms, to boot! I'm so happy, I want to pinch myself.

"Sunny, it looks so good on you!" Mickey says, tucking in the tag at the nape of my neck. "Did you see that Coach got our names embroidered on the sleeves?"

I gasp, noticing the *Sunny Park* stitched in silver on my cuff for the first time. "No way!"

Lindsey, who comes up behind me, laughs. "I reacted the same way the first time I got mine last year."

"These things always give me a wedgie!" Tawni yells, yanking at her new skirt.

"Stop complaining! We all have wedgies, but you don't hear anyone else whining about it, do you?" Shawni says, pulling her sister into a headlock.

The two are wrestling around the floor, but we're so used to their antics, no one even bats an eye.

The door flies open again, and this time Jadyn and Bea

come traipsing over in their perfectly fitting uniforms, pretending they're runway models.

"Mr. Reyes! Ms. Papadakis! Over here!" I say, playing along, pretending to be a paparazzi snapping pictures of them.

Bea lowers her imaginary sunglasses and gives me an air kiss. "Gorgeous, dahling," she says in a sultry voice.

Jadyn laughs, smoothing the sides of his sequined pants. "Watch out, world, the Dollies have arrived."

"You know what this means!" Lindsey busts out her phone. "Selfie time!" she says before taking a bunch of shots.

"Listen up, Dollies." Coach Tina looks fondly at us, like a proud mom. "Since you all did such a great job today at practice, and I'm in a good mood, how about we all go grab some pizza together at Giovani's. On me!"

YAYYYYY!

After we get permission and change back into our regular clothes, Bea, Jadyn, and I head out to walk across the street to the pizza parlor with the others.

We're chatting excitedly about the upcoming competition when I get an unexpected text.

It's Bailey.

Apparently, she finally had a heart-to-heart with her mom about how hard it's been accepting Darren and, surprisingly, her mom is being really cool about it. I guess they're going away on a trip to Catalina, just the two of them, to spend quality mother-daughter time together, and she wants to tell me all about it.

"Everything good?" Jadyn looks over to check up on me.

The traffic light turns green, and the rest of the team starts crossing.

"Yeah, everything is fine." The sun beats down on me as I stand there, texting Bailey about how happy I am for her.

Jadyn and Bea exchange a glance.

With an unmistakable saltiness in her voice, Bea asks, "Is it Bailey again?"

"Uh, yeah." I hesitate, rocking back and forth on my heels, trying to find a solution that'll make everyone happy. Obviously, I want to go to the pizza parlor with them, but I also know how huge this is for Bailey. She's been bottling up so much for so long, and this a major deal. "I just need a sec to make a call. Go ahead without me," I tell them, still thumb-typing furiously. "I'll catch up."

Jadyn's jaw tightens. "How do we know you're not going to cancel on us again?"

"What? No! It's just that Bailey's having this breakthrough with her mom and she needs to tell me about it," I say, over-explaining. "I'll talk to her for a little bit, then I'll come inside."

"What about us?" Bea says.

There's a beat of silence.

"Please understand, I'm just trying to be a good friend," I plead.

Jadyn's eyebrows furrow as he strokes his chin. "That's the thing, though. You're always running off to help her whenever she calls, dropping everything, but what about her supporting you once in a while?"

The muscles in my neck tighten up. "I don't always run off whenever she calls. . . ." I say in a quiet voice, more to myself than to them.

"Sunny, you literally left us high and dry that day we were making slime," Jadyn says, his tone clipped. "We had to stay up until ten at night to finish the order."

"I feel bad about that, but that was just once," I start to say.

But then Bea jumps in. "And remember last week, when we were cleaning out the PE storage closet for Coach Tina after school? You left a whole half hour early because Bailey called that time, too."

"Not to mention that time when you were late to practice because you were talking to her in the quad," Jadyn says.

"And that time you rushed us out of your house while we were eating chicken wings because Bailey was coming," Bea adds.

I didn't realize Bea knew what I was up to that day.

"We aren't saying that you shouldn't be there for your best friend, but you shouldn't have to flake on other people to do that," Jadyn says.

"Flake on other people?" I repeat. "Bea, is this how you feel?"

Bea nods. "I know you mean well, Sunny, but it sucks

that you're so quick to bail on us all the time. You say you want to be a good friend. Well, aren't we also your friends?"

Remorse comes over me. What they're saying is not wrong.

"I'm sorry, I had no idea you felt this way," I say softly.

This whole time, I've only been focused only on Bailey and what she needs, and I've never stopped to consider that Bea and Jadyn might need me, too. My role for so long has been Bailey's caretaker. I don't know how it became that way, but it has. Whenever she needs me, I listen. Whenever she needs to vent, I'm there. Sometimes she needs someone to take stuff out on. That falls on me, too.

I have so little time for other people I care about. I have so little time for me.

"I feel terrible," I finally say.

Jadyn's voice softens. "We didn't tell you this to make you feel bad. We just want you to know how it makes us feel, and hopefully you'll do better next time."

"Thanks. It hurts to hear, but I'm glad you told me." It would have been a lot easier for us to throw this under the rug and ignore it, but maybe it'd grow into something bigger over time.

"Me too," Bea says, squeezing my shoulder.

"I'll do better," I say, trying not to lose it in front of them.

"That'd mean a lot," Jadyn says with a sincere nod.

I put my phone away in my pocket. "I'll talk to her when I get home."

Bailey won't appreciate that I'm not replying right away, but maybe it's time I start listening to myself and what I want or need for a change.

✧ Chapter 29 ✧

The next week passes quickly, in part because Bailey is out of town with her dad at a family reunion in Texas. I miss her, but this time apart might be good for us. She can cool off about all the things she's mad at me about, and I can focus on dance team stuff and my handygirl job without having to feel like I'm in trouble with her.

In all honesty, the pressure of trying to balance Bailey with my new friends is starting to weigh heavily on me, and the lurking fear that my lies are going to catch up with me is making me lose sleep. I don't know how much longer I can keep this up. The only bright spot is the fact that the end is near. Regionals is only two weeks away, and the concert is another week after that. I've already made it this far. If I can make it a little while longer, then I won't have to worry about Bailey or anyone else anymore. Then I can finally be free.

I can do this. I have to.

At the start of practice, Coach Tina trudges into the gym with a grimace so serious, I know immediately that something is wrong. "Gather around, Dollies, we have to talk," she announces.

Uh-oh. This can't be good.

My teammates and I scurry to find seats on the bench.

"I've got some bad news to share with you," she says, propping one foot up on an empty folding chair. "I'm not sure if you've noticed, but Shawni and Tawni are not here today, and in fact they won't be joining us for the rest of the season."

My teammates and I look at one another with shock on our faces.

"Why?" Jadyn asks. "What happened to them? Are they okay?"

Coach slicks her hair back with her hands. "Luckily, it's nothing too serious, but last night I got a call from their parents. Apparently, they were on their hoverboards, messing around in the park, and somehow managed to break their arms.

A collective gasp arises from the team.

"Both of them?" Mickey asks, her eyes bewildered.

"Yes, I don't know all the details, but apparently, in true twin fashion, they broke one arm each." Coach squeezes her temples in disbelief. "How that's even possible, I'm not sure. But leave it to Tawni and Shawni to find a way."

My teammates look just as baffled as I am.

"Their doctor says they won't be needing any surgery, but they're going to be in casts for at least a month, which, as you can imagine, poses a problem for us as a team," Coach Tina says, cleaning the lenses of her glasses with the bottom of her shirt.

"Can't we just cut out their part from our routine?" Jadyn asks.

"Well, we could, but then it's almost guaranteed that we won't win," Coach Tina replies. "The bulk of our technical points in scoring came from their finale stunt. If you take that out of the equation, we don't really have enough to beat the East Valley Mustangs. If we're serious about advancing to state, we'd need to come up with something to replace their part. We may even need to switch to another choreography altogether."

"A new choreography? How can we switch to

something else at this point?" Lindsey says, biting a fingernail.

"Does this mean we might not make it to San Francisco?" Bea asks, her voice a bit wobbly. There's no doubt she's also wondering about how this is going to affect our hopes of going to see Supreme Beat.

"That's exactly what this means." Coach Tina sits down and sighs heavily. "I thought about our options before coming to speak with you, and I decided, due to this being a highly unusual situation, we should figure this out together as a team. The way I see it, we have two choices: We can either keep our routine knowing we won't win, or we can try to pull something together last minute."

Mickey drops her head.

Coach bends the bill of her visor with both hands. "Listen, I'm going to give you some time to discuss among yourselves what you want to do, and then we'll take a vote to see what direction we'll take from here on out. How does that sound?"

Jadyn, Bea, and I find one another in a quiet corner of the studio.

"I feel bad for the twins, but I also feel bad for us!" Bea says.

"Me too." Here I thought everything was in the bag. Each of us are getting so close to earning the money we need for our concert tickets, we practiced hard for our routine, everything was on track for our dream of seeing Supreme Beat to come true, and then this happens!

"Well, I don't know about you, but I've been working my butt off to see Supreme Beat, and I'm not ready to give up on all that so fast," Jadyn says, thrusting out his lower lip.

Bea wrings her hands. "Me neither! I've made enough slime to fill a lake—I am going to San Francisco one way or another. We just need a new routine."

It's silent for a moment as we rack our minds for a solution.

Suddenly, an idea pops up into my head like a slice of bread from a toaster.

"I've got it! Why don't we do the Supreme Beat song choreography we did at the mall? You know, without the dinosaur costumes, that is," I suggest.

"Do you think we could?" Bea says, mulling it over. "It's not exactly the kind of routine people usually do at competitions. . . ."

"Why not?" Jadyn says, visibly getting excited. "It's totally original, and we know it's a crowd pleaser!"

"Should we see what the team thinks?" Bea asks, clearly eager to share the prospect with our teammates.

"Sure!" I say right as the timer beeps, and we go to reconvene.

"So, any last words before we take a vote?" Coach Tina asks, gathering us together again.

Jadyn raises his hand and shares our idea with everyone.

"That K-pop song! I've heard it, super catchy," Mickey does a body roll singing "'P-p-p-precious.'"

"Yup, that's the one!" My heart does a little cartwheel because she's heard of it before.

"How does the choreography go?" Lindsey asks, looking skeptical.

"Should we demonstrate it?" Jadyn suggests.

"Uhh." I'm suddenly reluctant to do our dance without the dinosaur costume, but seeing Jadyn and

Bea's rock-solid confidence makes me swallow my fear. "Sure." What do I have to lose? We'll just show them and see how it goes.

The music comes on, and Jadyn, Bea, and I do the choreo, and when it's over, the response is mixed.

"Wow, it's certainly original. In a weird way. I don't know if that's a good thing or not yet," Mickey says, brutally honest as usual.

Lindsey looks doubtful. "How is your routine any better than the one we've already got? There aren't even any stunts in it. Wouldn't it be smarter to stick to the one we've been practicing?"

"If you think about the scoring card, two thirds of the points are based on projection and overall appeal," Jadyn explains. "With this routine, even if we don't score high in the technical portion, if we dance our hearts out nailing this very original choreo, we can clean up in the other two areas."

"Seems pretty risky if you ask me." Lindsey chews on a thumbnail nervously as she evaluates the options. "I've gone to state before, and no one was doing anything like this."

"All the more reason to try it—it'll be fresh, funky, and completely unexpected. Plus, we have the skills to execute this if we try!" Mickey says, her eyes blazing with excitement. "Imagine winning regionals with these clown moves—that would be the ultimate flex!"

Clown moves? Ouch.

"Mickey's right. If there's one thing the Dollies can do, it's dance our hearts out. We can make anything shine," says Bella, one of Lindsey's friends. "It's better than doing a routine that definitely won't win. This one at least has a chance."

"Let's do it!" Keira, another teammate, shouts, riling everyone up. "I've always wanted to do something different like this. The routines are all kind of the same—this one will definitely stand out."

We take a vote, and most of the votes are for the "Precious" routine.

"All right, if you all want to do it, I'll do it with you, but I'm warning you—you have to go all out or it won't work," Lindsey says, obviously still having reservations.

"It won't be easy to learn a whole new routine in such

a short amount of time, but it's worth a shot," Coach Tina says, putting her visor back on.

"Sunny, Bea, and Jadyn, I want you three to take over the role of team leader, since this is your idea." She claps her hand on my shoulder. "Until regionals, each of you will have to work overtime to master that routine. I'm talking every single day, ladies and gents. Be prepared to clear your calendars, silence your phones, ask your parents for a week off from chores, whatever you need to do, because we need to focus one hundred percent of our energy on polishing this routine. Capisce?"

"Capisce!" we yell back in unison.

And just like that, we're back in the game!

✧ Chapter 30 ✧

After some discussion, Jadyn, Bea, and I decided it would be best to break up the team into three main groups to teach the choreography for the new routine. That way, we'd be able to give detailed feedback and work on it as a whole group for the second half of practice. The choreography itself isn't hard, but it's all the tiny details that can make it tricky to execute with precision, especially with a group our size.

It seemed like a simple enough plan at the time, but now that I'm here in the thick of it, I'm starting to have second thoughts.

"You've got to be kidding me—robot dance moves?" scoffs Whitney, the teammate with a nasal voice.

My skin suddenly feels clammy. "That's the concept. It's dorky on purpose," I try to explain, but the waver in my voice doesn't exactly sell the idea.

"Sorry, Sunny, but you lost me." Mickey looks

skeptical. "I'm all for out-of-the-box routines, but it doesn't look *dorky on purpose*. It just looks dorky."

"Trust me; it plays well in front of a live audience," I say, but even I'm starting to wonder if it will without the whole inflatable dinosaur get-up.

"We're screwed," I hear Whitney whisper to Mickey when my back is turned.

Right about then, Coach Tina shows up. "How's the progress going, dancers? Let's see what you've got so far."

"Sure." I switch on the music and count us off, "Five, six, seven, eight!" but not even thirty seconds in, it all comes crashing down.

Not one person is on beat, and the form is a complete mess. My stomach burns with embarrassment. Maybe suggesting this routine for competition was a mistake.

Coach Tina leans down, pressing her hands into her knees. "Do you Dollies still want to go to state?"

We all look at one another, unsure if she's being serious. Her face tells us she's not playing around.

"This is not a rhetorical question. I'm really asking you, because we're in a tough situation with this whole broken-arm fiasco, and it would be understandable if we sat it out this year."

My mouth becomes dry, and I've lost the ability to speak.

Mickey answers first. "No, ma'am. We still want to compete."

Whitney and Keira nod also.

"Then I'm going to need you to commit to this one hundred percent." Coach Tina stabs the air aggressively. "Like it or not, this weird little dance is all we've got."

Weird little dance? This was certainly not the pep talk I was expecting.

"If we are serious about winning this, we don't have time to question style choices, we just have to go with it. The good news is that you're some of the best dancers in the state—you can pull off anything!" She looks us dead in the eyes. "But you have to trust the choreographers' vision."

She points to me. "As for you, you're the one who made up the choreography!"

I try not to shrink in her presence.

"You need to cut it with the sugarcoating bull

crunchies. These dancers can't read your mind. The only way this routine is going to come together is if you start directing them in a clear and precise way."

She's totally right. We don't have enough time for this. I have to get over my fear of offending them or we won't be able to learn this routine before the competition.

"Stop worrying so much about everyone's feelings." Coach Tina claps her hands loudly. "Tell them exactly what they need to work on."

My heart jumps, but I push through it. I have to, or I can kiss San Francisco goodbye. "Uh, okay, so maybe in terms of body alignment, make sure that your chin is lifted, your neck is elongated, and your eyes are off the floor. Whitney, in your grand jeté, your legs should be thrown to ninety degrees with a high jump. Right now you're only giving me half that."

I keep going. "Mickey, your form is solid up top, but you need to make sure your knees are relaxed, not locked. With kicks, your back should be straight, toes pointed, and hips level."

She stands up straighter and coughs into her fist. I might have heard a muffled *sorry* in there.

"Also, I'm seeing a lot of broken wrists in all parts of the routine. Use your plié instead of your arms to gain height." I demonstrate the move with proper form. "Or else it ends up looking really floppy."

"That's much more helpful, Sunny," Coach Tina says, thumping me on the back. "All right, now you know what to do. Get back to work!"

And miraculously, we do. Not just for that practice, but for the rest of the week. We settle into a rhythm where we basically live in the studio from the moment the school bell rings to when it gets dark outside. We do our homework on the benches between sessions, and a couple nights Coach orders pizza for us for dinner so we can squeeze in some extra practice. But somehow, Jadyn, Bea, and I manage to teach the whole team the new choreography, beat by beat, from scratch. To bulk up the routine for technical points, we even add a few more combinations based on suggestions from our teammates. It ends up being even zanier than the original, if that's possible. By the end, though, it's a perfect representation of who we are as a team, and I couldn't be prouder.

✧✧✧

After going hard at dance practice all week, I am completely wiped out by Friday night, but when I see Mom and Dad's car in the driveway, my heart leaps! They're back early from their business trip in Las Vegas!

"Mom? Dad?" I call, rushing inside the house to greet them. "You're here?"

"Sunny Bunny!" Dad picks me up and spins me around, and this time I don't stop him. "We skipped the last day of the convention because we missed you so much!"

"You did?" I say, touched.

"It's just a bunch of awards and boring speeches anyway. Did you do okay without us?" Mom asks, even though we've been FaceTiming every single night.

"Mom!" I groan, enveloping her with a bear hug.

She takes a good look around the house. "Everything seems like it's in its rightful place. Nothing is burned down."

"See, I told you we'd be fine," I tell her, finally releasing her from my grip.

Halmoni comes out of the kitchen with a steaming dish of tteokbokki. "Come, eat!"

We all grab chopsticks and crowd around the spicy rice cakes.

"After eating bland convention food this sure does hit the spot," Mom says, scarfing down a fish cake.

"So how did it go with Kiwanis?" I finally address the elephant in the room.

Mom's face crumples with disdain, and the mood of the room shifts. "Oh, that."

Uh-oh, maybe I should have waited for them to bring it up.

She takes a deep breath, staring down at her empty bowl. "Well, you can't win them all. Isn't that what they say?"

Dad rubs her back to console her. "We tried our best, though."

"You'll get them next time," I say, but then I spy Mom struggling to hold in a giggle.

"Just kidding!" she yells, throwing up both hands in triumph. "We got the contract! We finally beat C&C, and it feels so good!"

Both Mom and Dad jump up and start running around the living room, screaming.

"You did? Congratulations!" Halmoni says with a wide grin on her face. "You beat the C&C?"

Mom does a ridiculous victory dance, undulating her hips and pumping her arms like a wild woman. "That's right, baby!"

"That's great!" I shout, joining in the celebration. "I've got some good news of my own to share."

"What is it?" Dad asks, still dancing.

"Thanks to Mrs. Jones, I've officially raised enough money to buy my concert tickets!" I announce.

"WAHHHH!" Halmoni screams, jumping up and down with me. "That's my girl! I knew you could do it!"

The four of us are all giddily bouncing with excitement in a huddle.

Mom squeezes me tight, and Dad ruffles my hair. "I'm so proud of you, honey! You deserve it!" he says to me.

"Thanks," I say, pure joy radiating from my chest.

"Now all that's left is regionals." Dad winks.

Mom puts her arm around my shoulder. "How are you feeling about it, honestly?"

"You know what?" I take a moment to let it settle. "I'm feeling oddly good about it!"

"That's so amazing to hear." Mom squeezes her eyes shut and grabs her chest. "I know I'm being cringey, I'm sorry, but I'm just so proud of you, Sunny."

I feel a smile take shape on my face.

Her reaction doesn't gross me out the way it usually does, because this time it feels earned. Joining the dance team and somehow leading my teammates with a humongous choreography change at the eleventh hour hasn't been easy, especially for someone who's not great with change. For the first time in a long time, I'm proud of myself, too.

We hug in a Sunny Sandwich as I savor the moment with sweet satisfaction. Against the odds, everything is falling perfectly into place.

✧ Chapter 31 ✧

Later that night, there's a soft knock on my door as I'm about to climb into bed.

"It's open!" I call out, tying my hair up in a ponytail as I settle into my cozy comforter.

Halmoni comes in and sits on the edge of my bed. "You're still awake?"

"Yeah, what's up?" I ask, turning onto my stomach, pulling my pillow under my chin for a cushion.

"I came to tell you that I'm so proud of you," she says. "You have grown so much since you started dance team."

My chest feels warmed by her words. "Thanks."

"So strong!" She squeezes my knee affectionately.

"Just like you, Halmoni!" I reply, relieved that she's acting like herself again. "And now we get to go see Supreme Beat together soon!"

She squints like she's not sure whether to talk or not.

"Ah, actually, that's why I came in," she finally says.

I draw closer. "What is it?" I whisper, sensing it's some kind of bad news.

Her mouth pulls into a tight line, and her wrinkles deepen in the lamplight. "I'm so sorry, Sunny-ah, but I cannot go with you to the concert," she finally blurts out.

My lip trembles. This is what I was afraid she was going to say. All those signs I've been trying to ignore the past few weeks come flooding back to me. "Halmoni, are you sick?" My voice quakes, and tears spring to my eyes.

"Sick?" Her eyes bug out like I've turned into an alien. "Why would you think that?"

"I'm not a little kid anymore, Halmoni. I figured it out weeks ago." I sniffle. "The tiredness, the late-night calls to Korea. I know you've been trying to shelter me, but I'm not a baby. I can handle it."

"Oh, Sunny." She puts her warm hand on my cheek. "No, I am not sick."

My worries evaporate for a moment. "You're not?"

"No, I am in perfect health!" She flexes her biceps. "Strongest one in my Zumba class!"

"Then why can't you come with me to the concert?" I dare to ask.

She pauses. "Well, the reason is . . . I am moving back to Korea," she finally says.

"What?" Reality comes crashing down and breaks my heart into a million pieces. "Why?"

"Sunny, I am old, but there is still so much I want to do! Now that I don't have to take care of your grandpa, I want to travel and spend time with my sister and help out at the dance academy," she explains. "Don't worry, I will still come back and visit every year, and you can come to Korea to visit me, too."

"But . . . but . . ." I know I just told her I'm mature enough to handle bad news, but this is almost more than I can bear. "What about me?"

"Oh, Sunny. I will miss you so much, but you also have so many things going on here. Dance team and new friends and Supreme Beat concert. You will be okay without me. You are growing up, even got your period!"

A laugh slips out. "Halmoni!" I shriek with embarrassment.

"Just a joke, I'm sorry. I just said that to make you stop

crying," she says with kindness in her eyes. "I should have told you earlier."

I weep. "Do you really have to go?"

She tucks a stray strand of hair behind my ear. "Yes. You are growing up, and I am so happy for the year I could spend with you and your parents, but it's time for me to move on." She kisses me on the head. "But you are strong. I do not worry about you."

I sniff loudly. From the sound of her voice, I can tell that she won't change her mind. "When are you leaving?"

She looks down at her hands in her lap. "On November eleventh, the day after your competition."

I gasp. "That soon?"

"I know. It was my fault. I bought the ticket before you joined the dance team. I was supposed to tell you sooner, but I . . . How do you say . . . I chickened out," she says with a wry grin.

In my mind, my grandma is the most fearless person in the world, but I guess even she chickens out sometimes.

I exhale slowly. "That doesn't leave us with a lot of time, then."

She shakes her head glumly.

It goes without saying that I'm devastated by her news, but deep, deep down in my heart, I know it's for the best. Halmoni's whole life has been filled with adventures—who am I to hold her back from having more? She already missed out on so much while Grandpa was sick. As much as I'll miss her, I know moving to Korea will make her the happiest, and if that makes her happy, I guess I'm happy for her, too—or at least I will be eventually.

Now more than ever, I really want to win regionals! But this time as a send-off present for my grandma, who has given me so much of her courage.

✧ Chapter 32 ✧

When I walk into the convention center's main gymnasium for the regional competition, the vibe is electric. From the din of nervous chatter to the people rushing around like they've all had double espressos, I can tell it's not just me who's feeling it. There are clusters of dancers posing for pictures, proud parents looking over the program, and nervous coaches checking the time. There are so many people here, I feel like I've seen every style and color of uniform imaginable. I shudder at the thought that every single one of them will be watching me perform later.

Overwhelmed, I take a deep breath and give my stress ball a bunch of squishes, trying to quell the flutters in my stomach, as Coach Tina leads us to the waiting area in the competition arena.

I take a seat next to Jadyn.

"Don't worry, we got this," he says, clearly reading

the insecurity on my face. The sequins on his uniform sparkle under the overhead lights in the gymnasium.

My nerves, however, still run sky-high. It's not lost on me that how we perform today will determine whether or not we advance to San Francisco, which has come to mean so much for me and my teammates.

I smooth out the skirt of my dance leotard to steady my trembling hands.

We cannot mess this up. We are too close.

The judges are making their opening remarks when my phone starts buzzing in my bag.

I sneak a peek, and it's Bailey texting me again.

> **Bailey:** It's been forever since we've hung out! I have so much to tell you. Can you come over?
>
> **Me:** I'm at regional competition right now

The three dots that indicate she's typing appear for a moment but then disappear.

I wait and I wait, but a response never comes.

My heart sinks.

A simple "good luck" or a "tell me how it goes" or even an "I'll text you later then" would have been nice.

Disappointed, I turn off my phone and toss it back into my bag. I don't need this kind of distraction right now. I have to stay positive for the team's sake—and for mine.

Finally, the judges finish giving their opening remarks, and a group clad in soldier-inspired costumes files onto the dance floor.

My palms get sweaty with anticipation.

"Which team is this?" Bea scoots up in her seat.

"The Chonies," Lindsey says with a grim look on her face.

"Huh?" Jadyn elbows me for clarification.

"She means the Mustangs. It's a long story," I explain, thinking about Tawni and Shawni and how much they would have loved pranking their coach with Lindsey again. Too bad they're sitting in the general audience section instead of with us.

Jadyn laughs. "Oh, right. I heard about that nickname."

Bea shushes us. "It's starting!"

I hold my breath as soulful horns blare from the speakers, filling the auditorium with old-school jazzy feels.

The beginning of the Mustang routine starts out with some underwhelming choreography: the usual boring leaps, high kicks, and floor work. But then there's a deejay record-scratching sound, and the beat accelerates into a retro track with a mix of Tupac and Snoop Dogg and some other old songs I don't even recognize.

What is this?

Cheers explode from the stands as the dancers come alive, delivering some of the smoothest hip-hop moves I've ever seen.

"Not going to lie, that nineties-era throwback medley is genius," Jadyn says, bopping along with the song.

"They're totally pandering to the judges." I point out three judges sitting at the front table, grooving and singing along to songs of their youth.

All the confidence I had built up melts like ice cream on the sidewalk on a hot summer day.

The Mustangs finish their flawless routine and walk back to their seats with their chests puffed out like they own the place.

If Coach Tina is rattled by how good our competition is, she doesn't show it.

"We have to bring it big-time if we want to beat these guys," I mutter, and Jadyn and Bea nod in agreement.

We watch a few more teams come on, and before I know it, it's our turn.

Jadyn pulls me and Bea up out of our seats by our arms. "Let's just have a good time. That's what this dance is all about."

I hold a breath as we walk briskly over to our spots on the dance floor.

For a split second before the song starts, I close my eyes to focus, and the immensity of this moment hits me.

To me, this is no longer just about going to the concert. This performance is also proof to myself and everyone else that I am brave enough on my own. For so long, I relied on Bailey or Supreme Beat or my grandma to be my strength, but since being on this team, I learned that I've got some of my own strength, too, which makes me feel like I can be complete just as I am.

The power of that realization fuels me with boldness that chases away my jitters, and suddenly I'm eager to put it all out there, knowing that whatever happens, I'm proud of myself, and that's what matters.

As soon as the first few beats of "Precious" echo through the auditorium, my adrenaline spikes, and I let go. I dance my heart out, feeling the energy of this song that's brought me so much comfort and cheer through all of this.

I own this choreography that I created with my friends. I shake and groove, releasing myself from the things that have been holding me back: all the worry and self-consciousness and fear, they've got no control over me now. Not here!

The screams from the audience get me all fired up. I glance over at the others, and clearly our late-night practices have paid off, because we are putting on quite a show, swiveling and stomping in step with one another.

For the final sequence, the front row of our formation crouches and spins on their heads, which drives the audience completely wild. The auditorium is so raucous with cheering and clapping, I can barely hear the final notes of the song.

Over the sound of shouts and thunderous applause, Jadyn wraps Bea and me in a bone-crunching hug. "We did it!" he says, still out of breath from the grueling performance.

I laugh. We just performed choreography that included ninja kicks, the chicken dance, and head spins in front of an auditorium full of some of the most serious and polished teams in the region! For better or for worse, it was perfectly us.

We make our way back to our seats as the judges record their scores on their clipboards.

It's torture, but for the next half hour, we sit through the rest of the performances. Luckily, none of them, in my opinion, are as good as the Mustangs' or ours.

My chest tightens after the last team leaves the dance floor.

Jadyn, Bea, and I hold hands in solidarity when it's

time for the judges to announce the winner.

Even Coach Tina cracks her knuckles quietly in her seat.

It's the moment of truth.

A willowy lady with harsh eyeshadow takes the microphone. "Without further ado, we would like to congratulate the first runners-up. Let's give it up for the East Valley Mustangs!

My jaw drops. Does that mean . . .

"And for the champions of this year's regional competition, please put your hands together for the one and only Ranchito Mesa Dolphins!"

For a second, my mind empties and there's an expansive feeling in my chest. For months, I've been working tirelessly toward this goal, overcoming obstacles and putting one foot in front of the other, and now that I've achieved it, there's a lightness that springs from my heart, and I feel like I'm not even in my own body but up high in a hot-air balloon.

I did it. I actually did it.

I lock eyes with my parents and Halmoni, who are cheering from the other side of the gymnasium. Tawni and Shawni wave their non-casted arms at us. A lump forms in my throat, but then Jadyn and Bea pull me into the circle of teammates and we start jumping and screaming together. "We're going to San Francisco! We're going to San Francisco!"

I'm so happy, it feels too good to be true.

Unfortunately, I'm right.

✧ Chapter 33 ✧

Normally the sweet smell of waffle cone on a hot iron instantly puts me in a great mood, but today, not so much.

When Bailey invited me out for ice cream this afternoon, I thought it was to celebrate last night's big win at regionals, but she hasn't even mentioned it once. In fact, she hasn't even acknowledged the YAY! WE WON REGIONALS text I sent her yesterday.

I'm starting to think she's ignoring my dance team news on purpose to make a point about how little she cares about it, which really hurts.

"We stayed at the most awesome place in Catalina," Bailey jabbers away, describing their ultra-luxe beach hotel, not even looking at me as we get in the long line at Scoops Ice Cream Shop. "My mom liked it there so much, you'll never believe what she did."

Staring down at the red-and-white-checkered linoleum floor, I ask, "What?"

"She asked about their availability for weddings, and apparently they had an opening, so she changed the venue to there!" she says, pinching her lips shut. "I'm not even a romantic person, but I have to admit, this place is *so magical*. Can you believe her, though? So spontaneous! But weirdly enough, Darren was totally chill about it." She shrugs. "He still gets on my nerves, but if he can handle my mom and her wild impulses, then I guess he's not so bad." She's so wrapped up in her story, she's not even aware that I've stopped listening.

"That's cool," I say halfheartedly. Is she really going to go all afternoon pretending like we didn't win regionals? Is she that petty?

We inch up the line in front of the glass display freezer, and she hands me a paper menu. "Should we get the usual?"

I shrug. "Doesn't matter." I'm not in the mood for ice cream anymore.

"One large mint chip sundae. Two spoons, please," she says to the guy on the other side of the counter, and then she's right back to talking about her mom.

"Apparently, they were only able to snag the hotel because another couple canceled last minute, but now instead of getting married in August, they're getting married next Saturday."

"Wait, what did you say?" I jolt so hard, I nearly drop my spoon. "When did you say she changed it to?"

"Next Saturday. Why?" she asks, grabbing some napkins from the counter.

"Bailey, don't you remember? That's when I'm going to be at the state competition," I remind her as I follow her to an empty booth. "I can't come to the wedding if it's next Saturday."

"You'll be fine." The red vinyl from the booth squeaks as she plunks down into it. "I'm sure Coach Tina will understand. Everyone knows weddings and funerals are exempt from those team attendance rules," she says, nonchalantly waving her hand.

"No, no, you don't understand. It's all the way in San Francisco," I explain, suddenly feeling sick inside.

Her expression darkens as she turns to glare at me. "You're not going to get in trouble for going to a wedding, if that's what you're worried about. I promise, all you have to say is that you have a family event that came up. We're basically like family, after all." Her tone is matter-of-fact.

"I'm not worried about getting in trouble," I say, balling my napkin in my hand. "Everyone on the team is counting on me to be there. I'm one of the leaders, and we've been practicing for weeks for the chance to compete at this level."

Bailey spoons a big bite of ice cream into her mouth.

I take a deep breath. "Bailey, you don't understand. I want to go to San Francisco. I'm going to go," I say firmly.

Her eyes narrow in on mine, like it's finally registering that I'm not budging on this, not this time. "Are you being serious right now?" she snarls.

Her words grate on me. Why is this so hard for her to understand?

"Yes, I am." I can't look at her when I answer, but the snap in my voice surprises even me.

She says the next words extra clear so I'll understand exactly what she means. "Sunny, you realize I'm not asking you to go to the mall." She stabs her spoon into the mound of ice cream so hard, the sprinkles fall off. "My literal mother is getting remarried, and you of all people should know how traumatic this has been for me," she says, spitting the words in my face like an accusation.

I stand my ground. "I'm sorry. If it was any other weekend, I'd be there, but there's so much riding on this. I've worked too hard to miss the competition, not to mention the concert."

"Concert?" Bailey's head jerks. "What concert?"

My brain short-circuits as panic rips through me. "Huh?" I stammer, pulling back in my seat, but it's too late, the cat's out of the bag and it wants answers.

She clasps her fingers on the table, staring hard at me. "I had a feeling that you've been keeping something from me. In fact, I've suspected it for a while now. Now, tell me about this concert," she says with one raised eyebrow.

"It's not a big deal." I cover my head with my hands, suddenly flustered. "It's just a Supreme Beat concert that I'm going to in San Francisco with Jadyn and Bea after the competition, that's all."

"This is rich," she scoffs in disbelief. "My own best friend would rather go to a K-pop concert than be there for me in my hour of need."

I cannot believe her nerve! When it comes to Bailey, it's always about her, her, her! What about me? Why am I never allowed to need things?

"Bailey, this isn't just any K-pop concert," I try to explain. "It's Supreme Beat. Jadyn, Bea, and I have been doing chores and odd jobs for more than a month to raise money for these tickets. This is a big deal to us."

She takes a good look at me. "Oh, really? I thought that you were raising money for your team. Uniforms and budget cuts, right?" She rolls her eyes with a sneer. "Why did you feel like you had to lie about all this?"

"I don't know," I say, fidgeting with the spoon. "Maybe because you're always giving me a hard time about my music."

She lifts her chin. "So that makes it okay for you to hide it from me? For weeks?"

I have no response to that, so I keep my eyes down.

She shakes her head, disappointed. "Makes me wonder what else you've been lying to me about. . . ."

I gulp.

Her eyes flash, immediately sensing my weakness the way only a best friend can. "Tell me the truth. Did your parents really force you to be on the team?"

I hesitate. "Well, I mean, kind of, in a way . . ."

"Ugh! I should have known." She smacks herself on the forehead. "I had a feeling you were lying when you said that, but I didn't want to believe you would do that to me, so I trusted you!" she shouts, her voice strained.

Resentment that I've kept buried below comes ripping through the surface.

"You want to talk about trust? Let's talk about you." I drop my spoon into the bowl of melted ice cream and it lands with a loud clang. "You promised me that you wouldn't say anything about Bea's crush on Taylor Tang, and then you go blabbing it to him! I know you did, so don't even try to deny it," I say, my voice quaking with emotion.

"Sunny, I have no idea what you're talking about right now," she says, staring me down.

"Don't act innocent with me. You're the one who mentioned how she stalks him by the locker room, and then the next day he coincidentally stopped going that way. I'm not an idiot. I know it was you, Bailey. Just admit it!"

Her face crumples with hurt. "You can't be serious. You think I broke my promise to you?"

She can save her theatrics for someone else.

I double down. "I know you did. You're always trying to sabotage any relationships I make! Don't deny it!"

Her demeanor shifts again, this time to calm anger.

"Wow." Her glare penetrates my soul. "If you think I'd do that, then clearly we don't know each other like I thought we did."

"Maybe you're right!" My chest heaves, and my whole body burns with fury.

"Sunny Park, I feel like I don't even know you anymore. I have nothing else to say to you." She flings her napkin into the ice cream dish and starts to walk away, but then she stops in her tracks to add, “Get one thing straight: I’m not the liar, Sunny. That’s you.”

I look away.

“Mark my words, you are going to regret this,” she growls at me before she turns on her heel and stomps out of the place, slamming the door on her way out.

✧ Chapter 34 ✧

Hot with anger, I duck out of the ice cream shop as fast as my legs will carry me.

Without a real plan, I unlock my bike from the rack, pull on my helmet, and start pedaling hard down the street.

At this point, I don't even care where I'm going as long as it's away from Bailey.

Cars zoom past me in a blur as I whip through the streets, but all I see is red.

My thoughts are so jammed up with every kind of emotion, I cannot think straight. But one thing's for sure: I have nothing more to say to Bailey Stern, especially since she won't admit she broke her promise and told Bea's secret.

At least now I know for certain who my real friends are.

By the time I get home, I'm out of breath and drenched

in sweat. Before anyone can ask me any questions, I book it straight to my room, slamming the door closed.

Collapsing onto my bed, I glance at my phone, and there are unread messages from Jadyn and Bea, but I'm too flooded with emotion to engage.

I'll have to tell them all about this tomorrow, after I calm down.

Alone in my room, I lay my head on my pillow and let it all out until there's nothing left.

The next morning, I wake up with puffy red eyes from crying the whole night.

To my dismay, even after a face wash and a healthy dose of eyedrops, my eyelids still look like I got stung by a bee on both sides.

Lovely—just what I need in my life right now.

Who knows? Maybe no one will notice. That's the one perk of being a forgettable quiet kid in school, isn't it?

Unfortunately, as I walk through the halls of school, everyone seems to be whispering and staring at me. I don't know what the big deal is—haven't they ever seen someone who's broken up with their best friend before?

Desperate, I pull on my sunglasses before joining Jadyn and Bea where they're chatting in the quad.

"Hey, friends!" I call out to them as I approach. "How do you like my new shades?" I joke, trying to keep it light.

Bea levels me with a stare. "Friends? You think we're still friends? You're just going to pretend like nothing's happened?" There's a sharpness in her voice I've never heard before.

I whip off my sunglasses, aghast. "Bea, what are you talking about?"

Confused, I look over to Jadyn for an explanation, but he's scowling and his arms are crossed. He's like a different person; everything about him feels closed off and unwelcoming.

"Not cool, Sunny. Not cool," he says, looking down at his shoes, shaking his head with disappointment so stinging, it feels like someone doused me with rubbing alcohol.

"D-did something happen?" I ask, hiking my backpack up my shoulder.

This makes no sense. I haven't seen them since we

won regionals, and everything was fine between us then. Why are they acting like this all of a sudden?

Exasperated, Bea jabs her thumb in my direction. "Looks like she doesn't know yet."

"Doesn't know what yet?" I ask, frustrated that they're leaving me totally in the dark. "Will you please tell me what's going on?"

Jadyn runs his hand through his hair. "Try checking your Instagram," he says to me as they walk away together.

There's a rush of terror as I pull out my phone right there in the middle of the quad.

Fingers trembling, I open my app, and what pops up on my screen makes my blood run cold.

There's a newly uploaded video on my account that I definitely did not post.

With bated breath, I tap the thumbnail of my frozen face, and the clip begins to play.

It's an edited montage of me saying the most awful things:

Jadyn and Bea are just my teammates, not my friends.

Bea's laugh is so ridiculous, right? It's so embarrassing!

You know I'd never hang out with them if I had a choice.

It's only because my parents are forcing me to be on the team. Trust me, I would not hang out with them if it was up to me.

It's not my fault; it's Coach Tina who makes us practice all the time. She needs to get a life.

You know how the Dollies are [eye roll].

I can't wait to get my life back when the season is over.

White-hot rage spreads through my entire body as I realize that Bailey's been taking secret footage of me all these weeks, and she edited this to make me look like a monster!

My hands ball into fists. How could she do this to me?

Mortified, I take off running through the hallway, past the gawking faces and the snickers. I sprint to the only place I know I can have some privacy—the restroom in the library where Jadyn took me when I got my period. Once inside, I lock the door behind me and break down crying.

Overwhelmed, I sit hunched over, staring at the tiles on the wall, bleary-eyed and wondering how I ever got to this place.

Never in a million years would I think that my own best friend would stab me in the back like this. How could she do this after I trusted her with all my secrets? I get that she was mad at me for not telling her about the concert, but this—this feels unnecessarily cruel.

And to think, because of her, Jadyn and Bea had to hear all those terrible things I never meant for them to hear! She manipulated everything!

I'm so pissed off, I don't know what to do with myself, so I crouch alone in the bathroom for the entire hour, until I can get myself together enough to go to the office.

✧ Chapter 35 ✧

Mom barges into the nurse's office, frantic. "I came as soon as I got the call from the nurse." She rushes to my side. "Sunny, are you all right?"

I shake my head, blinking back tears.

Maybe it was an immature move to fake illness, but I'm so desperate to get out of here, I don't even care.

"Goodness, you look terrible!" Mom palms my forehead as she surveys my face. "No fever, though. I bet you got one of those nasty stomach viruses that are going around." A look comes over her. "Or maybe it's your monthly visitor," she whispers, her hand cupping her mouth.

I groan inwardly. Why is she like this?

"Don't worry, we'll get you home, maybe get you a hot-water bottle and a warm bath," she adds. "I think I have some Midol in the medicine cabinet."

"Please, I just want to go home," I say, grabbing my

jacket and backpack from the end of the cot.

"Of course, honey." Mom signs me out at the attendance office, and I can't get out of there fast enough.

When we get to the car, I unleash the flood of tears I was holding back. I'm collapsed in the passenger seat, sobbing so hard that I'm convulsing and gasping.

At a loss for words, Mom turns off the ignition and puts her hand on my back. "Don't worry, Sunny. This is all very normal; every woman goes through this."

"Mom, I do not have freaking menstrual cramps!" I bark, exasperated.

She pulls back, tucking her hair behind her ear. "Oh, I see." She doesn't say anything for a while. "Is this . . . Did something happen that triggered your social anxiety, honey?" she says tentatively.

Overwhelmed, I let out a scream that sounds more like a growl, which only makes Mom jolt with alarm. "I know—I'll see if I can get you an emergency appointment with your therapist," she says, feverishly scrolling through her phone. "Don't worry; we'll get you the help you need." The way she says it, the pity and helplessness in her voice, makes me snap.

My hands tremble with frustration.

When I catch my breath, I finally say in a measured voice, "Has it ever occurred to you that I may be upset about something that isn't related to my social anxiety?" I wipe my eyes with the backs of my hands.

Surprised, Mom turns to look at me. "What do you mean?"

My cheeks are hot, and my hands are sweaty. "I'm talking about the way you treat me! The way you baby me all the time. It makes me feel like you don't even see me as a human being. All you see is a problem. A problem you don't know how to fix. I wish for once you wouldn't focus so much on the things that are wrong. It's just a part of who I am, not all of it!"

She nods slowly, her own eyes watery. "I'm so sorry, honey. I had no idea you felt that way."

I look out the window on my other side. "Well, I do."

Mom frowns as she takes in the barbed things I've hurled at her.

Immediately, a surge of regret washes over me. I know there's no way for me to take those words back. "I'm sorry—" I start to say, but Mom cuts me off.

"No, Sunny, I'm glad you told me. I need to hear this." She comes close and touches my chin, her eyes zeroing in on me with fierce intensity. "I want you to know that there is nothing wrong with you. Look at me."

Reluctantly, I face her.

Her mascara runs as tears dribble down her face. "I'm so sorry if I ever made you feel that way. I promise from now on to listen without trying to fix you."

I nod, softening toward her.

She holds my hand in hers and squeezes so tightly, her knuckles turn white. "Now, do you want to tell me about what happened at school?"

My voice quakes, and tears fall down my face in sheets as I catch her up. I tell her everything from beginning to end. From how I lied to Bailey, to the incident at the mall, to the fiasco with the spy pen. By the end of it, Mom is so shocked, she's completely speechless.

"She betrayed me," I say, gasping between ragged breaths. "Why would Bailey do this?" I sniff, blowing my nose into a tissue.

"I don't know." Mom hands me another Kleenex, and I blot my eyes with it. This time she doesn't try to reassure me that everything will be okay.

I choke back sobs. "She's supposed to be my best friend," I say, my voice cracking.

Mom rubs my back with her warm hand, letting me make sense of my wild tangle of thoughts.

I wipe my hands on my jeans. "And now, because of her, I've lost Jadyn and Bea, too!" I'm so rocked with emotion, my body convulses into another wave of sobs. "Now I have nobody! Everyone hates me!"

My mom holds me as I cry into her shoulder. "Shhhhh," she says.

But it does nothing to take away the pain that's still searing inside.

Thanks to Bailey, there's no way I can show my face at school after this.

Worst of all, she's taken away what I really loved: dancing on the Dollies with Jadyn and Bea.

What am I supposed to do now?

✧ Chapter 36 ✧

Before school the next morning, I knock on the PE office door.

"Well, look who it is." Coach Tina scoots her desk chair over and opens the door for me. "Come on in."

Nervous, I sit in the empty chair on the other side of her desk, not sure where to begin.

"How can I help you, Sunny?" she asks, sticking a pen behind her ear.

I shove my hands deep into my jacket pockets. "Well, first of all, I don't know if you've heard, but there was a post on my social media—"

"Oh, honey, I know all about it," she says, cutting me off. "I think everyone at Ranchito Mesa has seen it."

I swallow hard. "Then I'm sure you heard the part where I said some not-great things about you."

She nods with a grim look on her face. "Yup, saw that."

"Well, I'm here to say sorry. The truth is, I didn't want my best friend to be mad at me for spending so much time at practice, so I blamed you for it so she'd get off my back." I take a deep breath. "It was really horrible of me to throw you under the bus like that. I want you to know that I actually really love coming to practice. If I could take back those words, I would."

"Not going to lie, that was a total butthole move on your part," Coach says, her mouth pulling down into a grimace. "Not a great look for you as a Dolly either. You know how seriously I take teamwork, and, I have to be frank, I was pretty disappointed when I saw that video. Not so much for me, but because of the way you treated your friends. Behind closed doors or not, that was uncalled for."

I look down at my feet. "You're right. I deserve that. I really messed up."

"You did. But I'll also tell you this: You are bigger than your biggest mistake."

She adjusts her visor. "Listen, Sunny, we are all human. We all mess up. In this day and age, sometimes we mess up big and it gets shared with everyone at school and sometimes the whole world. But the important thing is what we do when we mess up. It would be easy to hide and hope people forget. It's harder to be brave, own it, and pledge to do better."

This reminds me of what Mrs. Jones told me the day we cleaned her carpet: *Damage is still damage, whether we intend to cause it or not.*

Even though I never meant for Jadyn and Bea to hear those terrible words, I still said them. Yes, Bailey exposed me, but I should never have talked about my friends like that in the first place. They didn't deserve that. That was on me. I cared more about Bailey being mad at me than doing the right thing and standing up for my friends like I should have from the start.

But something's still holding me back.

My hands twist as I try to explain, "I want to take responsibility, but Jadyn and Bea are so mad at me, they won't even look in my direction when I see them on campus." My breath hitches in my throat. "I'm afraid they won't ever forgive me."

Coach Tina plants her hand firmly on my shoulder. "Here's the thing: They might not."

I glance at her, startled by her bluntness.

"But they also might. You'll have to give it a try and see how it goes."

She's right.

"I'm going to tell you something: Not all friendships last forever, and that's okay. Relationships are fragile, like a baby bird. You have to take care of it and nurse it when it's injured. Sometimes it heals and it's stronger for it, and other times, it doesn't make it. That's not how they show it in the movies, but that's how it is in real life."

The truth of her words sits heavy on my heart.

"But if you've hurt someone you care about and you want them to stay in your life, you have to do your part and take responsibility for your actions."

I bite my lip. "How, though?"

"It's simple, really. You reach out and tell them what's in your heart, just like you're doing with me right now." She rubs her chin. "You can't control what they're going to do with that, but at least you've opened the door and invited them in."

I shift in my seat, absorbing what she's saying.

"I know you'll do the right thing, Sunny. I believe in you," she says as she shows me to the door.

As I walk to class, I think about what Coach Tina said, and a clarity I didn't have before lifts the fog in my brain.

When it comes to Jadyn and Bea, it's easy. I know for certain that I want to remain friends with them. If it means that they might forgive me, I'll do whatever I can to show them how sorry I am.

But when it comes to Bailey, I'm not so sure. When she put up that video for all the world to see, she crossed the line. I messed up, too, and there's a lot that I can forgive, but knowing she was willing to hurt me to control me doesn't sit right with me. I deserve to be friends with who I want to be friends with and enjoy the things I want to enjoy, with or without her. I don't think she gets that. Even if she apologizes, I don't know that I could fully trust her again.

And, if I'm honest with myself, I'm not even sure how much of a friendship there is left to save. We've had so many good times together, especially before her family problems took over her life, but in the past year we've drifted apart a lot. Not only are we into totally different things, we're becoming different people, too. More and more it feels like we're forcing it to work when it's not. If I don't feel comfortable being myself around her anymore, maybe we've changed too much and it's time to let go.

I let out a deep sigh, and with it, I release so much of what I was holding inside, like a drain that's been unclogged.

It's hard to imagine my life without Bailey, but letting go of my expectations for our friendship makes me feel free in a way I haven't felt in a long time. I'm severed and sad, but another part of me is hopeful about being able to grow in my own way with nothing holding me back.

My steps quicken as I head to class.

From now on, I want to focus on the things that make me happy, too.

My mind races as I start thinking about ways to show Jadyn and Bea how much they mean to me. I have a few ideas, but I won't be able to pull them off without some help. I make a few phone calls, and luckily the people I ask are very supportive.

I don't know if this is going to work, but I am going to try.

✧ Chapter 37 ✧

A few days later, Coach Tina herds us to the side of the crowded auditorium. "Remember, Dollies, this pep rally is the last time we get to perform this choreography before we go to San Francisco this weekend, so we want to make sure it's perfect, capisce?"

"Capisce!" we shout back.

As we sit on the sidelines waiting to go on, I look down at my shoelaces, trying not to notice that Jadyn and Bea are sitting at the other end of the row, still not talking to me.

Hopefully, that'll change soon.

"Good afternoon, students! Welcome to Ranchito Mesa's fall pep rally!" Principal Jones bellows into the microphone. "It's such a pleasure to get together as a student body to celebrate all the positive things that are happening on campus. I'm sure you all know this, but our football team is currently undefeated." Everyone cheers as he gestures to the jocks who get up and give each other high fives and flex their muscles.

"And our very own Dolphin Dance Team came in first place at the regional competition last week!" he says, prompting another round of applause. "We're in for an extra-special treat because, in just a moment, they'll be performing the routine that brought home the blue ribbon for us. Before I call them up here, Coach Tina, will you introduce your team for us?" Principal Jones asks, handing her the microphone.

She grabs the mic. "Sure thing, Jerry.

"I gotta tell you, kids, getting this routine together has been a journey. I don't want to get into it, but trust me when I say that these dancers have had to overcome a lot of obstacles to bring home this win. But above all, I attribute their success to the tremendous camaraderie that's been built this year. It hasn't always been easy, and in fact, it's not easy even right now, but I'm proud that they're always working on being better."

She turns to wink at me. "Before we perform, one of the choreographers wants to share a few words with you about what this dance is all about."

A murmur rises from the crowd as I approach the stage. I'm sweating and my heart is beating wildly in my chest, so I take a slow breath through my nose before I take the microphone.

"Hi, my name is Sunny Park." I clear my throat. "Though you might recognize me from an Instagram post of me trashing my friends that went viral earlier this week."

I wipe my sweaty hand on my uniform, trying not to focus on the people whispering to one another.

Gripping the mic tight, I continue. "Anyway, the song we're dancing to is called 'Precious,' and it's about the value of friendship. This week, I learned the hard way how delicate friendship can be. Anyway, we've prepared a special video that will play as we perform. It's dedicated to Jadyn and Bea, who I owe a big apology to." I turn and look at them. "Hopefully, this video captures the way I really feel about you and the rest of the team."

I glance over at Coach Tina, who is sitting in the sound booth with a headset on. She gives me a thumbs-up as she turns on the projector.

My teammates glance at one another, confused, as

a huge screen lowers from the ceiling next to us. They look to Coach Tina for an explanation, but she swats the air with one hand, urging them to ignore it and perform as we usually do.

The song begins to play, and we start to dance, but as we do, pictures float onto the screen. They're a collection that Lindsey's been taking throughout the season. There's one of me, Mickey, Tawni, and Lindsey jumping up and down after winning the ice-breaker game during the first practice; one of the whole team stacked up in a human pyramid on the lawn outside the studio; there's one of Whitney and Jadyn doing homework on the gym bleachers; Mickey shoving a whole piece of pizza in her mouth at Giovanni's; Keira blowing out candles on a birthday cake; us in uniform holding the trophy at regionals; and one of us signing Tawni's and Shawni's casts. Even though I helped put this slideshow together, I get choked up seeing all the memories we've made this season.

Thankfully Lindsey picked up when I called her yesterday. Upon hearing my story, she actually agreed to help me put this together. For the sake of repairing my friendships and also for the sake of bringing unity back to our team.

At the end, just as the song concludes and we finish our routine, the last slide comes on the screen.

It's a picture of me, Jadyn, and Bea, laughing together while modeling our new uniforms. The caption at the bottom says **I'm sorry, please forgive me.**

After the screen goes to black, my teammates gather around me.

"Did you really do all this for us?" Bea asks, glassy-eyed.

I nod. "I know I really messed up, but I hope we can still be friends."

"We can," Bea says, grabbing my wrist. "This was really thoughtful. It means a lot."

"Come here, Sunny," Jadyn says as he and Bea wrap me in a big bear hug. "We forgive you."

Something I can only describe as sincere gratitude wells up in my chest. I know that I ruined things with Jadyn and Bea, and I'm so relieved that they're giving me another chance to make it right. "Thanks," I tell them from the bottom of my heart.

I look up, and there's not a dry eye in the audience. Everyone starts clapping and cheering as we exit the stage with our arms around one another.

After third period, I'm surprised to see Bailey waiting for me at the end of the wing for the first time since this whole drama started.

"Hi, Bailey," I say, trying not to be awkward about it.

"Sunny, that was quite a performance at the pep rally," she says as she approaches me. "I have to hand it to you—that was brave. It couldn't have been easy to pull that off."

"Thanks," I say, gripping the straps of my backpack.

"Anyway, I wanted to tell you that I've had some time to cool off and think about things, and I'm not mad at you anymore. We both got caught up in the moment and said a lot of stuff that I'm sure we didn't mean, and I'm totally ready to move on. As far as I'm concerned, we can just forget it ever happened."

I bite my lip, trying to figure out how this makes me feel. She's still never said sorry for betraying me and putting me on blast in front of the whole internet. I don't think she really understands how much her actions hurt me. More than anything, I'm not confident that Bailey is going to be any different than she was before.

"I got you and your grandma something." She reaches into her backpack and pulls out two Supreme Beat beanies. "It's for your concert. I hope you have a great time."

"Thanks, we will," I say, taking them from her. "That was really nice of you. I'm sure my grandma will love it, too." After spending a heinous number of hours on the phone with her travel agent, Halmoni was able to move her flight back so she can go to San Francisco with me after all.

Bailey smiles, but I can see she's still got sadness in her eyes. "I'm going to miss you at the wedding, but I understand that you've got your own stuff to do, too."

I reach out and squeeze her hand. "That means a lot to me." It really does.

"So, you want to go get some ice cream after school, then? I have to tell you about this drama club I'm auditioning for," she says, already edging toward the cafeteria, but I don't budge.

"Actually, I can't. I'm meeting up with my dance team friends then," I tell her. "But please tell your family hi for me at the wedding."

"Sure, uh. Yeah, I'll do that," Bailey says, nodding.

I wave, and we head our separate ways.

✧ Epilogue ✧

"We are with our people!" I announce.

My body is practically vibrating with energy the moment we walk into the crowded concert venue. All around us, fans of every age, shape, and race come streaming through the aisles, carrying light sticks, signs, and armloads of Supreme Beat merch. Some even came with huge banners with the members' faces plastered on them.

"This is exactly what I dreamed it'd be like," Jadyn says, looking around the stands with his mouth agape in wonder. Huge LED screens play old Supreme Beat music videos as people make their way to their seats.

"Hang on," Bea says, slowly panning her phone 360 degrees. "Do you see this? Isn't it incredible? I wish you were here with us," she says into the phone.

Next to her is Halmoni, who is clad head to toe in sparkly purple Supreme Beat gear. She pops her head into the frame of Bea's FaceTime conversation. "Hi, Taylor!" she says, waving to him. "Sorry, but Bea has to go enjoy the show now."

Bea just laughs as Halmoni takes the phone from her. "You talk to your girlfriend later, okay? Don't worry; we will take care of her."

Embarrassed, Taylor coughs into his fist. "Yeah, so sorry. I'll let you go, babe. Call me later!" he says, blowing Bea a kiss through the screen.

"Bye, I'll miss you," she coos, taking back the phone in one hand and flipping her hair with the other before hanging up.

Jadyn, Halmoni, and I make barfing sounds.

"Don't be haters. I can't help it if I'm in love," she says, making finger hearts. "I'm sorry, Taeho." She kisses his face silk-screened on her T-shirt. "I'm a taken woman now."

A few days before we left for San Francisco, Taylor finally worked up the courage to ask Bea out. Bea was shocked, since she thought he was avoiding her in front of the locker room. Turns out Taylor was going the long way because he was afraid he had BO. I guess Bailey never blabbed the truth about Bea's crush after all. Go figure.

Things between Bailey and me are a little weird, and we're still figuring it out. We're friendly when we see each other, but we're not texting or hanging out as much as we used to, especially since I started eating lunch with Jadyn and Bea and she started sitting at the table with the kids from Drama Club. Knowing we probably won't be as close as we were before makes me sad, but I think it's for the best—for both of us.

Because of this concert, Jadyn has found a new calling. Even though he doesn't need to, he's still working at his mom's hair salon on weekends. He started an Instagram account for his hair creations that's become a hit. Even a few of our teachers from Ranchito Mesa have gone in for a blowout with the friends-and-family discount. It was the randomest thing, but last week Brenden Sylvester's mom came in for a highlights refresh. Jadyn said she was the nicest lady ever. Not that it makes up for her son's sucky behavior, but at least Jadyn knows he can tell on Brenden straight to his mother if he ever needs to.

State competition was an experience. After lots of hugs and kisses from my parents at the airport, we arrived with Coach Tina and the team in San Francisco. It was loads of fun flying in an airplane and staying in a hotel with my teammates. Coach Tina made us go to bed early, but we managed to get in an epic pillow fight before lights-out. We woke up early and competed our hearts out. Unfortunately, we didn't end up placing in any of the top rankings, and we won't be advancing to the next round of competition, but we put on a great show and made a lot of people laugh, which felt like its own kind of win.

And just before we got to the concert, Halmoni helped facilitate a flash mob that we've been organizing online for weeks. I still can't believe we pulled it off! Strangers we've never met in real life gathered at the designated location, in front of the concert entrance a couple hours before the show, and we danced to three whole tracks together. Maybe if it goes viral, Supreme Beat will see it and laugh. Who knows?

Halmoni being Halmoni packed little boxes of kimbap rolls and mandu for everyone who showed up as a little thank-you gift. I'm going to miss her so much when she moves to Korea next week, but I already have plans to spend the whole winter break with her, so it's not too bad.

It's funny—I started this whole journey with the Dollies to make Bailey happy, and somehow found myself and the ways I need to make myself happy, too. I'm so glad I put myself out there, even when I didn't feel brave enough. Being part of this team has helped me to rise above my biggest worries and step into the life I want to have.

My skin tingles all over as the stage lights come down, and I hold my breath in anticipation. I can't wait for the amazing things I'm about to experience.

ACKNOWLEDGMENTS

To my editor, Joanna Cárdenas, thank you for giving me the time and space to figure out the heart of this story. Your insightful questions never cease to draw me deeper into my characters, unlocking so much more substance and meaning from what was there before. I owe so much of this story to you.

To the entire Kokila family (Namrata, Jasmin, Zareen, Sydnee, Gnesis, and Asiya) for bringing stories like mine into the spotlight. Thank you for your commitment to diversifying the shelves, one book at a time. I'm so proud to publish with you again.

To the folks at Penguin Young Readers, this book is for you: Caitlin Taylor, Maria Fazio, Tabitha Dulla, Nicole Kiser, and Ariela Rudy Zaltzman. In the School and Library team: Carmela Iaria, Venessa Carson,

Summer Ogata, Trevor Ingerson, Rachel Wease, and Judith Huerta. Shout-out to the Digital team: Lauren Festa (I love our video!) and Tolani Osan. Thank you, Christina Colangelo and Kara Brammer, in Trade Marketing. My appreciations for Todd Jones and Nicole White in Indie Sales. To Kim Ryan and her Subsidiary Rights team, thanks for making my Scholastic Book Club dreams come true. I could not do any of this without you.

A giant hug for my publicist extraordinaire, Kaitlin Kneafsey, who moved heaven and earth to make this book and *Stand Up, Yumi Chung!* shine even during the scary early days of the pandemic. I will be forever thankful for all your effort.

To my agent, Thao Le: I tried to stop writing this book more than four times, but you wouldn't let me. Thank you for being my strict Asian auntie and making me finish it. You saw potential in this even when I did not, and I can't thank you enough. Forever grateful.

A great big thank-you to Masae Seki for capturing Sunny's and her friends' spirits so well in the cover art!

Shout-out always to my writer-sisters, the Kimchingoos. Thank you for being beside me always, every step of the way. I lobe you, Susan, Grace, Graci, and Sarah.

To Kellie Elmendorf, my writing partner who has been with me from the very beginning. Thank you for helping me find the heartbeat of this story. It took me years and many, many attempts to unearth it, and I wouldn't have been able to do it without your honest advice, comments, and suggestions. This book is so much fuller because of you.

To my family, for putting up with all my whining and supporting me anyway. You are the best.

To Phil: You're my number one, my always and forever best friend. Thanks for being you.

To my late halmoni: I thought of you so much while I was writing this book. When I can't pull together enough strength of my own, I remember yours and it keeps me going. I love you and miss you so much.